I, From Nothing
Isabel Tallysha-Soares

Translation by Isabel Tallysha-Soares
Translation editor: Marcia R. Prior-Miller

To my Dead from Nothing.
To my nephew, Manuel, and my niece, Margarida,
so they know we come from Nothing.
To Pedro, who joined us, the heirs of Nothing,
and believed...

I, From Nothing
Isabel Tallysha-Soares

All rights reserved. No part of this book may be reproduced, stored in a retrieval system or transmitted in any form or by any means electronic, mechanical, photocopying, recording or otherwise, without the prior permission of the publisher.

ISBN 978-1-903110-66-9

First published in this edition 2021 by Wrecking Ball Press

Published in Portugal by Coolbooks (Porto Editora)

Copyright © Isabel Tallysha-Soares

Book design by humandesign.co.uk

All rights reserved.

The People of Nothing

Genealogy of the Owners of Nothing
|
Grandmother (founder of the Candeia)
|
Son
|

Isabel from Nothing	(m. Boschoff, first name unknown)	Younger sisters
	(d. during the French Invasions)	

|
Son of Isabel & Boschoff
|
Grandson of Isabel & Boschoff
|
Great grandson of Isabel & Boschoff
|
Great-great grandson of Isabel & Boschoff (m. Argentina)
|
Américo, Great great great grandson of Isabel and Boschoff (d. 1930, m. Sabina)
|
Máxima, "My Mother", Daughter of Américo and Sabina (d. 1963)
(m. Manuel Tibério, "My Father", later Manel[1] from Nothing (d. 1943)
|
Matilde, commonly known as Luísa,
Daughter of Máxima and Manel from Nothing (b. 1911)
|
(m. Antero de Novaes, d. 1967)
|
Issue by Matilde (Luísa) from Nothing
|
- from António — António (d. in infancy, 1936)
- from Ángel Aguirre (alias, Ordoño Güellar) — Bela Flor (1941, stillborn)

The Other People of Nothing

- Romano, Manuel Tibério's brother (d. April 9, 1918)
- Margarida, Manuel Tibério's sister (d. 1918)
- Engrácia, Luísa's nanny (d. 1955)

---

[1] Manel is the usual, informal name that Manuel assumes in everyday Portuguese.

DETAIL MAP, NOTHING, PORTUGAL

Preface and Acknowledgements

I, from Nothing was originally published in Portuguese as *Eu, do Nada*, the title, a literal translation to the English. It is based on the true story of a family who named their farm "Nothing" and who have lived in a so-named place for over two centuries.

The toponym "Nothing" has been subject to academic and journalistic scrutiny. Curiosity as to how and when the name came into existence are exemplified in an article published in the 1990s by a renowned Portuguese journalist and polemicist, Miguel Esteves Cardoso. In 2014 another Portuguese journalist and TV host, Pedro Rolo Duarte (d. 2017), challenged me to write the story of my family in a novelistic fashion that could reflect the country's history from the early 1800 onwards and thus *I, from Nothing* was created. My first words of gratitude go to him and his insistence, a memory that will always prevail.

My second words of gratitude go to my Portuguese publisher Porto Editora and my editor, Vítor Gonçalves, who took a chance on a first-time novel writer and have since encouraged me to keep writing and publishing.

If this book crosses the borders of Portuguese and finds its way to English-readers, further thanks belong to David Abrahamson. He urged me to share my English translation of *I, from Nothing* with Marcia Prior-Miller, who served as translation editor for the manuscript, capturing both Portuguese culture and mores, and a story, moving from one non-related language to another. To her, my gratitude for the path we have walked together to get here.

The English rendering of *I, from Nothing* also owes to the enthusiasm of its first readers. I am grateful to Barbara Buzan; and the members of the GLC Book Club in Iowa, U.S.A. (Allison Eness and Mark Taylor; Jerry and Nancy Rabe; Weldon and Pam Abarr; Karen Jensen; Margot and Paul Eness; and Tom and Sharon Prochnow), for their comments and encouragement; as well as translation editorial assistant, Christina Prevette, who compiled club member comments and reading notes for the final English translation edits.

Last but not least, one is only a writer as long as there is a publisher. To Shane Rhodes I owe the catapult allowing this book reach the broader public of English as a global language. In a saturated editorial market, he has successfully been steering an independent publishing house whose catalogue is a testament to the wonder(s) of slow Literature and slower Poetry all the while taking a bet on emergent, mostly unknown authors. No words can adequately verbalise the honour and privilege it is that *I, from Nothing* finds a place in the elegantly curated catalogue of Wrecking Ball Press. To Dave Windass, assistant editor, and the people at Human Design my gratitude for all the efforts and commitment which shaped this book to life.

I, from Nothing was only possible because of the inspiration I got from the lives of my Grandmother Luísa, born Matilde in 1911, my Greatgrandfather Manel from Nothing and my Mother upon whom the main characters of this novel are based.

Nothing, December 4, 2020.

I
(Prologue)

Despite their being unexpected, I had been waiting for them. It was not long after the Revolution when they came. Questions. They had questions but were not interested in the answers. Weird times . . . when freedom and democracy were released from the cage of imprisonment and went on to ravage the land, and that meant being modern.

Obviously, I did not show them the tombs, the vaults I had built when you made your spectacular entrance for the second time, just as I did not show them the fenced lake I erased from the map when I wanted to kill you. O, how I wanted to kill you . . .

We have always puzzled them. The wise wanted to reduce us to academic theses and theories, in the belief they had found an explanation of us. As if finding an explanation enshrined them in the grandeur of knowledge. And their theories and irrefutable ideas were better and more real than our existence or what has brought us here. I let them think so. I let them think their theories reflected their Science and that their truth was the Truth. I let them be in their petty lives of the science of nothing. The meaninglessness of knowledge makes me laugh.

The others, the journalists, wrote of us only because they found us a curiosity. Maybe they were drawn to us because they thought we were ridiculous in our rural ways; silly because of our name, always our name, and because the people find particular enjoyment in awkward, strange names. Cosmopolitan, they looked at us from above.

I did not mind. After all, we were the country, the landscape, the back of beyond, or worse, the province. I also let them be. Like Science, the press loves to create truths. We are what we are and that is the only unchangeable truth, one that neither theses nor articles can comprehend.

Interesting, Death. It also makes me laugh now.

In the end, I have always died more each time I died until the day I stopped feeling my own death and was born. In the void of me, my soul got used to living amongst shrouds and vaults and the knell of bells. It may well be that this whole now is simply my inability to distinguish between here and there, and therefore I carry on living, opening the doors to one side and the other, oblivious of where I am. Here, we have always negotiated time and space with the naïveté of someone who does not know in what exactly they are trading. It was only natural for us.

I see you standing in that corner and watch you linger on in that long indecision that takes up your days. You just stay still in the calmness of the suspended time which fills this room, the study that has survived the ages.

Dead or alive, it was from here that I commanded the time that, for decades and decades, gave life to this everything. I owned a time of sowing and harvesting, an ever-repeating cycle of time that I sometimes harnessed and that, at other times, overpowered me, and that, more often than I care to remember, brought me down to my knees.

I was your middle woman, a mediator. But those days are over and you now keep me company. You have become so familiar you do not frighten me anymore. There you stand. Shapeless and bleak. Motionless beneath the three black swallows of Bordallo faience[1] that Mother had placed on the wall before I was born. Are you tired of all the years and all the toil? Or are you just patient? Do you thank me for my labours by sparing me from you? Or are you taking your time in making me your heiress? You do not seem as vigorous as you used to be when, irrespective of seasons, you reaped seedlings which had barely been put to freshly ploughed soils. I saw your heinous grimaces and never imagined you could shrivel down to become this

---

1. Raphael Bordallo Pinheiro (1846-1905) — A famous Portuguese, multi-talented artist best renowned for his socio-political satirical cartoons and his life-depicting works of art in classic Portuguese faience, a variety of porcelain with a vitreous tin-glaze, usually profusely decorated. The Bordallo Pinheiro faience is known for its plates in the shape of cabbage leaves, decorative swallows and other earthenware objects imitating plants and animals. It is still very popular today and much used for decorative purposes.

emptiness I see before me. Or maybe it was my eyes that changed and have gotten used to you as we eventually get used to everything. Pain fills us with habit and we find it strange not to feel it when you go some other way and leave us alone momentarily. Such is our habit: to feel awkward in the presence of happiness, for it is a hiatus, an impossibility of being possessed permanently. Maybe I have grown accustomed to you, or maybe you have grown weary of me. What do I know?

You do not react anymore. There, where you spend your time in a limbo of waiting, was where the seamstress used to visit us. Do you remember? You keep her near, I am sure. We would hear her pedaling at the machine. The sound had the mechanical rhythm of sewing. Sometimes a thread needed cutting and the sound subsided; then it was back to sewing again, and the rhythm resumed its course for more stitches. I thought I would never hear it, and I still do not know how you let her escape. In all likelihood, it must have been Mother who called her for company. Yes, you also let Mother escape. But, as always, she only responded to her own will and did not linger here for long after she died. She went away and took the seamstress with her. Even the werewolves that gave off sparks under their hooves on the stones of those lonely roads disappeared after she left us.

In the irony of so many presences, we are all that is left. Everyone else is gone. I have remained here, spending my nows in this study accompanied by the diaries in whose pages faithful pains have been written down and alleviated. I have been left here to atone for my life, as if I had to pay for freedom.

There they are, the diaries, locked in the bookcase that is carved into the thick wall of stone and white plaster. They rest there in piles, yellowed by time, tied with ribbons that were once pink. They are insulated behind doors of thin, parched wood and panes of fine glass of bygone eras: a glass brittle and gently rippled, made at a time when things were imbued with the soul of their makers.

The thick red silk curtains behind the glass panes were put there at Mother's order: she who loved the books to which she related better than with us. She had the panes covered so the books could be protected from direct sunlight and live forever in their original colours. The last thing she wanted was her books to have their souls sucked out by light and time, the way we have our bodies sucked out by light and time. She immortalised both their physical existence and their spirit, and that reminds me of the irony of our mortality. They are there still: Silva Gaio's *Mário*, in a first edition[2]; *Nau Catrineta*[3]; the early Pessoa[4]. And the magazines: the *Crónicas Femininas*[5], which she kept without my knowing why; and the newspaper clippings that seemed important to her, some of which I remember, others whose meaning is unfathomable to me.

And there they are also, my diaries, added to those piles of other words, neatly written down on reams of paper sewn between leather or cardboard covers lined with silk paper that time and moths have meantime chewed. Indeed, it was she who gave me the space in the bookcase when she discovered I wrote diaries, and it was she who tied, with pink velvet ribbons, those notebooks I wrote while she lived among us without being among us.

"The bottom shelf. You may use it," she told me one day before the study was mine. Before Nothing was mine.

I did not know her to be a woman of affection. The gift of that shelf was perhaps her life's greatest expression of love. And that day I decided, if not to love her, at least to try to find something that made us mother and daughter. I had nothing similar to give her in return. I had words. But what are words that die out in the air in comparison with the tangibility of that shelf rescued from the holiest of holies

---

2. *Mário*, by António da Silva Gaio (1830-1870) — A novel published in 1868, depicting the nineteenth-century conflict opposing the Liberal and Absolutistic factions in Portugal.

3. *Nau Catrineta* (literally "Caravel Catrineta") — An anonymous poem narrating the perilous sea journeys of Portuguese discoverers in the sixteenth century. In the mid-twentieth century, the name *Nau Catrineta* was used to title a collection of books with texts highlighting the Portuguese spirit as a seafaring people who conquered a great empire. The Fascist dictatorship ruling the country at the time used the books as propaganda.

4. Fernando Pessoa (1888-1935) — One of the greatest bards of the Portuguese language and the epitome of the Modernist movement in Portuguese literature.

5. *Crónica Feminina* — A magazine founded in 1956 for a feminine readership. It included columns for good housekeeping, a section about celebrities and high-society parties and events, and was known for the inclusion of serialised photonovelas or photo *feuilletons*, that is, magazine sections devoted to fiction, criticism, or light literature, with stories photographed as if they were cartoons and plots usually of impossible love.

the woman possessed in this life? One shelf. A whole shelf set aside for my diaries. One shelf taken from Mother's precious bookcase, and given to me, a stranger in that room and a stranger to the bookcase.

I, I have always been one for saying words. I have always blown them away in the wind and expelled them from my chest, sometimes even before becoming aware of them. I only took to writing them in black on the virgin paper laden with possibility when life came storming through the door to take me with it.

She, on the other hand, was not one for wasting words. She read them in silence. That mute pronunciation was her language. All my life I knew her that way: quiet and verbally frugal.

I never quite understood why Father, a man of many utterances like me, had chosen her for his bride. It surely was not because she was the heiress of Nothing. Father was not the gold digger type.

It was said she bewitched men with the strangeness of those icy eyes. There had been a suitor who threw himself into a well. The people said it was because she did not want him.

However, Manuel Tibério, with his heart of peace and words that came easily, fell in love with her on the day he saw her debut at the ball in Ladeirinhas[6], the village from whence Nothing drew the hands that made it an everything. Immune to the cold spells cast by the eyes of the only daughter of the owners of Nothing, he determined to leave for Africa as though he were a convict if he could not have her.

He had her.

By that time, her father had almost lost hope of seeing her marry. A reputation of beauty and ice haunted her, scaring away suitors in the same measure as it attracted the love of men.

She was choosy and whimsical, they said. And then, they added, she behaved thus because she was far too vain and thought too highly of herself on account of knowing how beautiful she was. She was neither a candidate for nor recipient of sympathy. People whispered, with a whiff of contempt, that women like her aged to be

---

6. Ladeirinhas, pronounced *Lah-dey-ree-ñas* — The Portuguese "nh" sound is the "ñ" sound in Spanish, as in "España", or the French "gn" sound as in "montagne".

spinsters, and that would serve her right! But the one thing on the peoples' tongues that most marred her reputation was the hushed rumour that she saw and heard things: translucent, blond children playing next to bales of hay (a little boy and a toddling baby-girl, they said); the sound of the ghost seamstress sewing at her machine; and shadows of nothing appearing out of the long, hair-like, lime-green algae undulating in the clear water of the stream meandering peacefully at the lower-end of Nothing. All of those things, topped by her almost colourless blue eyes, lent the daughter of Nothing the strange aura of a different woman who was probably better left alone inside the great house of Nothing.

Her father did not know how to drive off the rumours and, faced with the agony of his wife's tears shed as she died more each day because her daughter was passing the age for marriage and child-bearing, thanked Providence for Manuel Tibério to have come along with his genuine interest in that gossamer light woman with hair the colour of stubble fields in August.

They were married with the pomp and circumstance imposed by the status of the ownership of Nothing, the strongest farm for miles around. The chapel of the estate was decorated with myrtle and wild broom flowers, and the Priest of Vila Franca was called in to officiate the wedding. Her father was the epitome of jubilation. He had pigs and cows killed and paid for a reception to live in history. He invited everybody he knew, and there was no cellar big enough to accommodate the board tables he had set in front of the large barrels with the year's wine.

His daughter did not join in the party. She did not take to the populace, and the people reciprocated that dislike. She preferred to stay in the banqueting room of the big house where the guests of higher standing were treated to their own reception.

On that day it became clear that, more than marrying his daughter off, my Grandfather Américo had gained a son. And that is how Manuel Tibério, better known as Manel in the manner and fashion of the land that reserved the Manuel for the formality of the Registry, became Manel of Nothing.

They were always very close, my Father and my maternal Grandfather. They went together to the cattle markets in Cartaxo. They left for the fields at early dawn, shared their lunch with the ploughmen and returned home by dusk, not yet tired by a whole day of talking to each other. It was unimportant to my Grandfather that his son-in-law was the son of the owner of a small plot of eastward-facing land. Perpetually confronted with the mild, rising sun and the quickly growing shades that descended over it after midday, the vineyard always yearned for the powerful, grape-enriching sun of the afternoon which kissed other vineyards and brought wealth to other pockets. A piece of land divided in two by a public way between the upper vineyard and the lower, so small the family could hardly make a living. Consequently, there were many days in the year when Father's father was nothing more than a hired man working for whoever needed muscle to toil the fields. Grandfather Américo thought nothing of the humble origins of his son-in-law. Important only was that Manel had a heart of gold. And for that reason, Grandfather called him Son with a warm familiarity he did not have with his own daughter.

Helpful and friendly, easy smile on his lips, only a man like my Father could have married my Mother and not succumbed to madness. Only a man like my Father could have married my Mother and not perished from the grief with which he would henceforth live his days.

I was born in 1911, the year of the Orthographic Reformation.[7] Other countries had one for religious purposes; we had one so that the "ph" in Pharmacy could be changed to a less conspicuous "f".

---

7. Orthographic Reformation — In 1911 the government passed legislation to simplify the Portuguese language and to bring some convergence between oral and written speech. Prior to the 1911 reformation, the language followed the Latin and Greek etymons in the writing of words, so the underlying intention was to modernise written speech. Words such as "Pharmacy" were modernised to "Farmacy," with the "ph" sound, which existed alongside the "f" sound, expressed only by the letter f. Similarly, words such as "lyrio" (lilly) replaced the "y" with "i" to become "lírio". In 1990, a New Orthographic Reformation, implemented to align the several variants of Portuguese (European, Brazilian, Angolan, Mozambican, Cape Verdean, Guinean), has met with intense public and political antagonism. Not all Portuguese-speaking countries have ratified it.

Two years had elapsed since my parents had married and my grandmother Sabina had meantime died. It was as if she had just been waiting to see her daughter settled in life so she could leave hers. This passing away meant my Mother was now the Mistress in the house of Nothing, a mistress only in presence because it was really up to Engrácia, my nanny, to manage everything domestic.

I think I let my Grandfather down when I was born. Maybe he thought that because I resembled my mother physically I would also be as strange and moody as she. He was forgetful of the fact that I also resembled him and all them of Nothing since the day Nothing had become Nothing. But Father took it upon himself to raise me as the heir of Nothing. His mission in life was now one of making me inherit that whole everything. He knew there would be no births to follow mine.

He closed his heart to Mother, thus giving her all the space her tortured soul needed. A widower of a living wife. He set his mind and strength to Nothing and to my upbringing and from then on they started to live in separate rooms. Mother considered her child-bearing duties fulfilled. There were days on end when she did not leave the space between her bedroom and the study where her precious shrine of books was lodged: this same small room, facing the vineyards and the stream, which I call office because of all the letters and words inhabiting it and that I inherited from her when she let herself die of nothing in 1963.

Now, after all the generations are gone, I look to the corner where you stand staring at me and waiting to be overcome by the wish to take me. For all the length of the wait that is keeping you from taking me, I presume I must have given you so much trouble that you now wonder what to do with me. Or do you mourn me? It is always like this when I go to bed late at night, for sleep has also forsaken me, and loneliness keeps me the company of me.

You stand there: quiet, still, and resting from all the years of hard labour. I do not fear you. Maybe we are locking horns to see who is stronger. Tomorrow I will have a couch put there so you can sit while you relax or make up your mind. We will be two old women talking to one another. You know everything that ever happened to me, but you never managed to reach deep within me. You looked at everything from the outside. Shells. All you saw were shells, and I pity your ignorance the same way I pity the ignorance of the wise and the journalists who tried to put us into words. At last, I live well with you. Perhaps you have become a habit.

I look at the white layers of brittle mortar that paint the walls of this study. I never let anyone paint them with anything other than the quicklime that produced a hissing sound wrapped in billowing smoke while it was being molten in big buckets of water. It was during summer that the thick, cool walls of the house, the House of Nothing, were painted. What a destiny! To inherit Nothing so that it becomes nothing.

Once there appeared a Frenchman asking about Nothing. A wise man. He was carrying out some academic research about improbable toponyms and had come to know about Nothing. He came sometime after the Revolution and told me, as if I did not know it, that this was the only place in the world that was called Nothing. The nothing which is something. The supreme irony of the existence of nothing. I told him the story just as I tell it each time someone asks me why Nothing bears this name.

II

I think I can tell you, not what you saw, but my version. The time of Nothing is long. Long of what it was. Long of what it is. And time is nothing to us.

You hear the sound of hooves on the gravel. Tired horses, panting and chomping the bits. You remember, of course. It was known that they would come; it was only a matter of days. Eerily, no voices are heard. They have come to plunder and occupy. They have been marching for miles and miles and want to get to the capital. They are exhausted.

"Arrêtez!" The command goes out and the sounds of steps of worn-out leather soles and hooves fade in a collective halt. The door is flung open by a violent kick that breaks the lock, ripping it from the frame while wood splinters fly into the air.

The grandmother and the girl freeze with fear.

They stayed behind when the owners left, taking with them the oxen, the mule-pulled carts, the servants, the roosters and the rabbits caged in big wicker baskets, to seek shelter behind the trenches of the Lines of Torres. The parents could not take the grandmother who was crippled by old age. She would only delay them, and it was imperative to save the children. The eldest of the granddaughters determined to stay with the grandmother. Maybe because she did not identify so much with her infant sisters, born as they were out of time when time begged for a son, a male to perpetuate the blood; or maybe because she was too fond of her grandmother. Or maybe because, after all, as an elder sister, she felt she had to protect the little ones by staying behind to try to save the farm.

The French had arrived.

They were there, impudent, tramping on the varnished pinewood floor of the sitting room, scratching it with their spurs and the dirt of conquered roads.

Those must be the officers. They had to be, for arrogant were their manners and the way they fell heavily onto the chairs. The saddle had tired them. Yes, those with the petulant manners were officers, the owners of regimental power.

There were other soldiers who searched the house, opening the chests and the closets. They did not acknowledge the two women. Just shoved them aside as they went by, while asking with gestures and grunts of an incomprehensible language whether there was food and drink in the house.

Holding each other as a Siamese body, the women both nodded in the affirmative. All they wished was to be left alone. The soldiers could turn the house upside down. They could take the wheat in the big chest in the kitchen.

The chest which is still there, in the downstairs living-room, having survived the eras and the salt of stored dried cod, is the chest where we keep the wedding dresses of the brides we were.

Well, let those soldiers empty the amphorae where we stored the olive oil; let them find the earthen pot with the lard where preserved chunks of pork were left so the girl and the grandmother would not starve. Want and starvation were unimportant to the women as long as nobody separated them.

Let the French do as they pleased and move on. Let them not linger here in the Candeia.[8] They could destroy at will, as they had done at all the other farms. Grandmother and granddaughter did not care: They would rebuild everything. Let them be unharmed in that corner of the corridor between the kitchen and the sitting room. The officers could sleep in the bedrooms on the upper floor and soil the sheets with their stinking, soggy sweat full of the fine dust of the gravels of the roads of the vanquished country they were crossing. When they were gone, a strong lye of ash and soap would be made, the sheets soaked in the mixture, taken out to dry in the sun, and their whiteness would be restored. And so would life. Just let them go away, voracious French animals for whom no gallows nor pillory could ever serve justice.

---

8. Candeia — Pronounced Kan-dey-a, means "oil-lamp".

Beyond the Lines, things were no better. We obeyed the English, who, in their esteemed posture as colonisers, treated us as illiterate and dumb colonists. They expected gratitude for saving us, all the while robbing us in broad daylight, leaving us defenceless—we who did not even have our Court in the country.

We were dying by the thousands, of typhus and dysentery in the infected, muddy trenches which, or so it was hoped, would protect the capital. Soldiers and the humble people quartered in an amalgamated mass of filth and all vicious things that come to pass when hordes are cramped together. There was starvation, and there was fear. Those who had left their houses and the lands of the ancient in search of sanctuary against the invaders did not know whether there would be a return home.

The forts of the Lines of Torres were nothing more than towers strategically placed on top of the rugged hills surrounding the valleys near Lisbon. In nearby Carvalha, Cego, and Serra de Alrota, the hills that circled the valley made an east-west barrier against the Invasions coming from the east, precisely where Spain was.

The forts were there: Star-shaped walls of mud and stone, whose moats had been dug on the flanks most exposed to attacks. Three or four hundred soldiers strong and half a dozen cannons each, they were our only hope to thwart the Invasion. The steep topography upon which they had been erected was, however, the best protection the forts had to offer. It was to those Atlantic wind-swept heights of tenacious, bushy vegetation that the frightened inhabitants from the farms and villages of the west converged.

Seen from above, that is, from the hills encircling Sobral, Bucelas and Arruda, the farms in the Warm Valley seemed placid: The lush greenness of the vineyards lent a deceivingly idyllic peacefulness to the landscape below. The French were there, scavenging houses, barns and crops like rabid jackals in a pack.

The Candeia was just another wine-producing farmstead deserted in the flight. Nobody could anticipate whether, after the war was over, when all the fugitives would come down from the hills, the grandmother and the granddaughter would still be there, or whether they would be found spared and alive. A thousand deaths would be preferable to a life tainted by shame and the horror of indignity, for how could the girl live with the spectre of humiliation? The grandmother had refused to leave. Her bones were sore by the proximity of death, and the Candeia was her whole life. Isabel had stayed with her grandmother.

The French went away as quickly as they had arrived. That night they had slept at the Candeia and wreaked havoc in the place. The next morning they left, laden with the wheat they found in the chest. They spilled the oil of the amphorae all over the floor and left it there, fouling the air with its rancid smell which stuck, dense and greasy, to one's nostrils and clothes. Even the limp mule, worthless for the escape of the owners of the Candeia, they took with them.

Their booty was bountiful: the cuckoo clock; the ivory blessing crucifix which hung on the wall overlooking the master bed; the silver candle holders, and all the knick-knacks they could get their hands on in the big house of the Candeia.

They broke furniture and set the stables on fire. The hay their horses had not eaten was thrown into the well for sheer evil. They devastated, destroyed and ruined everything they had no immediate need for.

Wells were left empoisoned or silted up with all kinds of garbage and waste. Even holy places were gutted: All the chapels and churches met the cruel ravages of desecration. In the small village of Fountain Ireira,[9] they chopped the hands off of the patron saint for the silver of which they were made. And everywhere, they pillaged the gold-flaked, carved wood of the altars. Decades later we started hearing about the Lusitanian relics on display in Parisian museums. There was no record in history of such indecencies in our land of peace and long-established borders. The French were worse than the Barbarians.

But war, you know, has never been known for refinement.

---

9. Fonte Ireira — Pronounced Font *Ee-rey-ra*.

When, at last, the scavenger packs went away, the owners of the Candeia were welcomed back by the girl, spared as well, like the sacrificial lamb from holocaust. Old age was in their bodies, made weary by starvation and hopelessness. The daughter awaited them. Their only remaining daughter. The little ones had succumbed, too young and frail to survive the disease-ridden, death-filled trenches.

The old woman was alive too. Devastation had summoned her strength, and she seemed less crippled than before. The Candeia had survived. The wounds were licked and life resumed its course.

A year had passed since the last Invasion of 1810[10] when the foreigner appeared at the gates of the Candeia. He did not speak much Portuguese. He was tall and pale, and his eyes were of a never-before-seen translucence. He had gone back to France with the demoralised contingents of an army he had been forced to join, and all for nothing.

Three times had Napoleon sent his armies over the Iberian Pensinsula in the glorious hope of getting to the Atlantic. But Portugal stood in his way, and three times his armies were defeated. The bloodshed was for nothing and a glorious hope became an inglorious chapter in Napoleon's ambition and the beginning of his fall.

The foreigner longed for the warmth of the southern, meridional latitudes, and his mind kept remembering a farm located between the Montejunto, the highest mountain in the vicinities of Lisbon and the Tagus River. No sooner had he arrived in the motherland than he turned back to the Atlantic West he knew to be Portugal. He walked for days on end, sleeping under the stars and eating whatever he could find, when and if he could find anything. His soul was soothed when he glimpsed the distinctive, rectangular shape of the Montejunto.

He had arrived.

This time he had come in peace. It was not like when he had

---

10. The Invasion of 1810 marked the last of the French invasions into the Portuguese territory by Napoleon's armies. The First Invasion was in 1807, the Second in 1809 and the Third in 1810. The Portuguese refer to this period as the French Invasions.

scoured that land in the company of his hungry pack. From the foot of the mountain it was easy to see the tranquil, mighty blue river, and his senses told him he would find his way to the farm between the lazy river and the mountain. Serendipity had taken him to a farm whose name he ignored on a dangerous night of invasion. For some reason he could not put into words, he had noticed a girl holding fast to an old woman. Her hair was disheveled, but her eyes were bright with fear and determination.

Now, standing at the gate, he understood what it is like to miss something so much it could almost hurt. Hardly did he know that the language he would soon speak forever as his own had a specific word for that, *saudade*.[11] In that moment, his heart sank at the thought of the possibility of what might have been when a helpless girl is left to face the unbridled manhood of soldiers in the heat of war.

His name was Boshoff, the name that has remained with us ever since, together with the water-like eyes and the hair of ripe wheatfields, all of which are going to die with me. He married the girl and, from then on, we are Portuguese nicknamed "the Russians": long-legged, thin and blond.

Soon after, the government issued an order that all properties should be officially registered. When the surveyors came along to check the boundaries and corner markers of the Candeia, it was the Frenchman, now a husband and a father, who showed them around. He let them see what they had to see, but when he got near the stream, he raised his arm and indicated to them there was nothing beyond. The surveyors marked the stream as the southern limit of the Candeia, ignoring completely that the bulk of the farm lay precisely in the place to which the Frenchman had so clearly pointed.

He then went to the Registry and had a land deed issued under his name, baptising the whole property Nothing. And Nothing it

---

11. *Saudade* — Pronounced saw *thatha*, means "a nostalgic longing for someone or something that was lost and is deeply missed."

became. Because there was a huge mortgage on the Candeia, on account of the money the father of the girl who was now his wife had needed to rebuild the farm after the ravages suffered at the hands of his countrymen, the Frenchman thus found a way to redeem himself. If ever the mortgage could not be paid to the bank, the Candeia which would be lost would not be the original farm but only a tiny fraction.

As you see, as in all cosmogonic myths, we were born from chaos. But, contrary to myths, our chaos had a name, and it was from that name that Nothing was born. The Nothing we are of plenty.

The Frenchman had a son who inherited Nothing, who, in turn, had a son who had another son who had yet another son. Then came we: my grandfather Américo, my Mother and I, although I think my Mother was really nothing to Nothing. The true heir of that generation was my Father, who rescued us from the collapse it could have been had my Mother been in charge of Nothing: a farm of toil and sweat, cornfields, vineyards and orchards. If there had not been Father, Mother would have run away or died of the death she died decades before she did die. Neither would I be here to tell the story.

III

Father had a younger brother, Romano, whom I barely knew. I remember his kneeling in front of me one day and removing some stray hair from my face. His eyes were so profoundly sad.

But maybe it is my imagination playing tricks, attempting to understand his eyes after knowing what happened later.

Romano looked like my Father: the same hazelnut eyes, and he, too, wore his thick brown hair cut very short at the back of his head. People said Romano was a wild ass. Father protected him by giving him work on the farm. It was his attempt to keep the slandering tongues of the people at arm's length from his brother. Those were the same tongues which talked about Mother's strangeness.

One day I wanted to know what an ass was. I had overheard something about asses that were neither asses nor donkeys, and I thought I had heard Uncle Romano's name. And that was several years after the day he had knelt and gently brushed the hair from my eyes. So, one morning, before my lessons, I asked Engrácia. She was braiding my hair, getting me ready to go to the room where I had classes with Mademoiselle Mirabelle, the private tutor hired to educate me at Nothing. Mother did not let me attend school in Ladeirinhas, and Father opposed my going to boarding school at the College of the Saint Slaves in Lisbon. She did not want me raised as a simpleton; he did not want me far from his love for me.

"Those aren't things for a young lady!" Engrácia answered and hastened to finish the braid, pulling a few threads of my hair in the process, which made me cry "Ouch!" and quickly put my hand to salve my bruised scalp.

For a ten-year-old, a no was a word pregnant with promise, for it was perfectly clear that the things not suited for a young lady were definitely things a young lady had to know.

"Come on," I insisted, "I can hardly recall Uncle Romano, but I don't remember his looking like a donkey."

"All set," Engrácia said swiftly and helped me rise from the chair in front of the mirror. "All set for your lessons!"

It took me days of insisting until Engrácia capitulated when I threatened to ask Father what on earth was an ass, and why was my Uncle one?

I learned more than I could have ever anticipated, and for a long while after that I was scared of blowing out the candle before going to sleep.

To be an ass was to be a werewolf.

Asses were men who changed into wild beasts resembling asses. On certain nights they gathered on the crossroads of lonely roads and, apart from that, little was known of their activities other than they roamed mindlessly about. Sometimes vegetable gardens and threshing floors where grain was winnowed would appear all trampled over in the morning, and people knew they had been there.

In the villages there would be at least one man who people suspected of being an ass. The men could even have normal families, but rumours stuck, and they were said to be lost souls facing a fate of eternal punishment from which they could not escape. It was not that they wished to be asses, it was simply some sort of atonement to be borne, and that was it. Asses were cursed, and nobody knew why. And, as far as my Uncle Romano was concerned, all I had to do was believe that people were foul-mouthed fools.

Hesitantly, I asked Engrácia whether she believed in werewolves, and her affirmative gave no solace to my fears, but fired up my fertile pre-adolescent mind, which wanted to know more and many things about the world outside the borders of Nothing.

Uncle had served in the Great War. He joined the Portuguese Expeditionary Corps, embarking from Lisbon and arriving in Brest, on the westernmost point of France, where the French have their Finistère, or land's end. It was 2 February 1917. The war was still far, very far, from being over.

I know this, because my Father never forgot the dates associated with his brother. I was already six then and can vaguely recollect a farewell at the train station in Vila Franca.

It is one of the very few images I have of Mother outside Nothing. That particular occasion was imprinted in my memory. She was lean and stood very straight, which only added to her height. And she was wearing an ankle-length emerald dress trimmed with black satin lace, which afforded a glimpse of her spool-heeled shoes. She always stared into the distance, and we were never able to tell where or at what exactly her hard eyes were looking.

That day I saw her in a context of strangers; I compared her to the rest of the people and thought her different. Not that I found her beautiful. I did not even know what beautiful meant. Beautiful was Engrácia when she took me with her to the fountain at the bottom of the gentle slope leading to the stream; beautiful was Princess, Mother's copper-coloured mare. There, at the station, I thought Mother had an aura that distanced her from us.

Crystallised in that memory, I barely remember Uncle Romano going to war.

Dear brother,
We arrived well and have already received our marching orders.
Don't let our mother fret over me and tell her I'll be there soon.
Give my regards to everyone. Your loving son and brother,
Romano
Brest, 3rd February '17

Mother kept all the letters. All the ones she received and all the ones we received at Nothing.

Uncle Romano's, which are few and scarce in words, she tied with a white lace ribbon, which became brownish and dotted with rust stains over time. In the knot, she placed a dried *Pelargonium* flower[12] that must have been scarlet and is now the colour of old blood (so appropriate, come to think of it). I imagine her re-reading the letters after the events that were to come.

---

12. *Pelargonium hortorum*, also known in Portuguese as *sardinheira*, is a flowering plant of the *Geranium* family. Red and orange *sardinheiras* are very common in gardens and balcony pots throughout Portugal and very typical of Lisboan historical neighbourhoods.

Dear brother,
Our Commander says there was a meeting today with Lieutenant-General Haking and we will be relieved the day after tomorrow. Count the days to my return and tell our mother her son is coming home. Give a kiss to your Tilda, who must be all grown by now, and send my love to everyone. Yours,
Romano

Lys, 7th April '18

Tilda. My Uncle called me Tilda. Curious. I have never heard my name said by anyone else, except Mother. I was Lizzie for Grandfather Américo, Luísa for Father, My Child for Engrácia, and Miss for Mademoiselle Mirabelle. Then, when I grew up, I became the Daughter of Manel of Nothing, to finally emerge on my own as Luísa of Nothing.

Only Mother called me: Matilde.

For many years I thought my name was Luísa and it was only upon my First Communion when the Priest asked for my birth certificate that I discovered my real name was Matilde, just as Mother called me, and not Luísa, as everyone else used to call me. Because Mother was Mother and the only one to address me thus, I had grown up under the assumption that she had given me for a nickname the name of one of the fugitive heroines of the novels she read.

As it turned out, when I was born Father wanted me to be called Luísa, but Mother insisted on Matilde. I was baptised Matilde, but Father never gave in and, for him, and after him, for everyone else, I am Luísa. I sign Matilde despite looking at her in the third person, a distanced I, unknown even to myself, the remote memory of Mother and the strongest link binding me to her.

When they come for my dead body, I want them to call me Luísa, Luísa of Nothing, and I wish Matilde to live only on paper.

"Here lies Luísa of Nothing, who signed, forgetful of herself, Matilde Boshoff," you can write for my epitaph. And you, how do you call me? Have you gotten used to Luísa, or do you regard me as Matilde?

The news came before Uncle's last letter. The telegraph boy from Vila

Franca arrived in Nothing, all sweating and out of breath. He had an urgent message. There had been a great battle, a terrible butchery, and Uncle had been killed. There were no other details. Things were made clearer when Chico da Aurora and Zé Carlos returned from the war. But by then it was too late to hold Father back.

On hearing his brother had died, Father took Baio, his faithful Lusitanian horse, and vanished. No one knows where he went, but he must have stopped in all the taverns and cellars of nearby wineries, because when by nightfall he arrived at the public house in the centre of Ladeirinhas, where people were already talking about the death of Romano and the bell was knelling for the death of a son of the land, he was not himself.

Like black ravens, the old women had, in the meantime, flocked to the house of my other grandparents, as nothing provides better distraction to a community than a nice disgrace abundantly watered with tears. Father, of usual a man of cordial words and serene behaviour, had thundered through the door of the tavern in a state of soul that only the pain of mutilation and the red wine could explain.

"Are you happy now? Are you?", he hollered in anger. "So many times did you call him an ass that he ran away. You only know how to speak behind a man's back. Cowards, all of you! You've killed my Margarida, who was only a child, my God! Bastards!"

And he wept and raised his arms up in the air and screamed they had killed his brother and his kid sister.

As a matter of fact, Father had never forgiven those people for the suicide of his sister. Aunt Margarida had told a friend she had been kissed on the mouth behind the church. Suddenly, a swift straw fire broke out in Ladeirinhas, and it was burning on people's tongues that Margarida was dishonoured, and there could be nothing worse than a woman's reputation going from mouth to mouth. When they pulled her out of the well, they saw she had tied her skirt between her legs with the bobby pins from her bun. She did not want to be seen undone when it was her lifeless body that was pulled out from the still, dark water of the well in the upper vineyard.

"Cowards...", sobbed Father, prostrated on a chair of the tavern when the energy of his fury began to wane. "Cowards... Stop saying my wife is weird," he muttered, his face a contorted mess of tears and slobber. "She isn't weird. Leave her alone . . ."

At that moment, Father had reached that cathartic moment when, like the wounded wolf before the pack, he summoned his remaining strength to exorcise the demons of evil-saying that haunted his family and shattered his heart: Uncle Romano, Aunt Margarida, Mother.

Uncle lost his life in La Lys. Without a body to bury, Father gave money so a military cemetery to honour fallen soldiers could be built inside the cemetery in Ladeirinhas, and he had Mass said for Uncle's soul every Friday for a year. He wore black until his dying day, whereas Mother, in her usual way, made a pile of clippings related to the battle.

It was a cruel irony of fate that the Portuguese contingent was going to be relieved on the very day that German forces charged and *decimated it on 9 April 1918.*

It must have given you tremendous pleasure knowing that Uncle wrote to us saying he was coming, and the letter got to us with him dead and buried in a distant land.

You sure were busy in those days.

Uncle's Commander in the 8th Battalion, Major Xavier da Costa, was blinded and wounded three times before being captured, and hundreds of Portuguese soldiers lost their lives on that ill-fated day. Nevertheless, the most infamous thing was, as Zé Carlos and Chico da Aurora later explained, that the English, our ever faithful, well-intended allies, thought it our fault we had lost the battle. Out of sheer cowardice, they said.

As a punishment for what they thought had been our indiligence on the battlefield, they gave our boys the inglorious work of digging trenches and repairing roads. Their intended punishment saved the 1st Division's lives. Had our men not gone back to the Front, we would not have marched down the streets of Paris in the Victory Parade on 14 July 1919.

From those clippings Mother collected, I learned the toll. On the unfortunate Western Front alone the Portuguese Expeditionary

Corps lost 2,160 infantry, 5,224 were wounded, and 6,678 were taken prisoners.

For this family, Uncle Romano is the martyr of the Great War, the vain sacrifice we made so we could keep Africa for a few more decades.[13] Father never forgave the Republicans for the death of his soldier brother. He said that had it been in the times of His Majesty, Dom Manuel and his mother, Her Majesty Dona Amélia, the country would not have gone to war in a subaltern position to the English. It was, he said, the lack of backbone of the Republicans in that confusing array of Government after Government that characterised the First Republic.[14]

He always longed for the reinstatement of the Monarchy and, until his death, he kept a white and blue flag of the olden days in the chest of the Invasions. When a new dictatorial Republic took over in 1933 under the misleading name of New State, Father would never let his beloved flag out of sight, for fear Nothing might be searched for anti-fascist items. Several times he stored the flag in different,

---

13. Portugal entered World War I when its African colonies were threatened by German forces. There were no battles on Portuguese soil, and the Portuguese Government took on a belligerent role only when Angolan and Mozambican territories bordering German West and East Africa were invaded. Active Portuguese military involvement in the Great War was carried out by sending contingents to the battlefields of France and the then Portuguese African colonies. The Portuguese Republic's main objective was to safeguard the colonies from German invasion, which would mean losing them. In the 1960s and 1970s, however, African independence movements would lead to the formal loss of the colonies.

14. In 1908, King *Dom* Carlos and Crown Prince *Dom* Afonso were shot to death by Republican supporters. The King's second son, *Dom* Manuel, where *Dom* is Portuguese for "Sire," used to address the royals, took the crown but managed to stay in power for only the next two years. On 5 October 1910, a Republican *coup* overthrew the Monarchy and the Royal Family fled to exile in England. The Republican regime was only four years old when it was caught up by the events of World War I, which further added to its struggle to achieve political maturity. In fact, in the aftermath of the institution of a Republican regime in Portugal, there followed a period of political turmoil as presidents and governments alike failed to stay in power long enough to finish their terms.

Portugal's participation in the First World War was on the side of the Allied Forces because Portugal and Britain share the world's oldest, still standing Alliance between states, the Windsor Treaty, signed in 1386. Under the treaty, whenever one of the signatories is in danger of attack, the other comes to its aid. Besides the Alliance, the young Portuguese Republic entered the war as a means of strengthening its claim to power in the eyes of the other European monarchies.

La Lys was one of the bloodiest battles of WWI, with the Germans heavily defeating the Allied forces and the English assuming it was because the Portuguese had not fought bravely. In all these centuries of Alliance, the Portuguese feel they were never treated as equals by the English: that the Alliance has only served to safeguard British interests, not the Portuguese.

unsuspecting places, but nobody ever came to Nothing in search of flags and signs of loyalty to other regimes.

You never snitched on Father and I thank you for that.

And, for yet another most cruel irony of fate, Father also blamed the Republicans for the death of his parents, soon after Romano's.

When the Spanish influenza got here, in May 1918, the family was mourning the recent and overwhelming loss of the soldier son. Many people in Ladeirinhas contracted that deadly pneumonic flu.[15] Many survived the illness. My parental grandparents succumbed.

That year my Father lost his family. All the blood he had left, apart from me, was a sister who was a housemaid in Lisbon and a brother, a priest in Alpiarça.

Had his parents not been so weakened by the suffering of losing child after child, one killed in action, the other taking her own life down the well, they might have found the reasons to ward off the disease. As it was, their spirits were so broken that death was welcome. Therefore, in the eyes of my Father, had it not been for the Republican regime, which had overthrown the Monarchy in 1910, his family would not have gone through all that pain and misery.

I still pass by the picture of Uncle every single day. His is the sepia photo of a soldier in a rigid pose and sad features on the mantelpiece of the living room. My Uncle, who, people said, was an ass and who called me Tilda.

A long many years later, when we finally began to lose Africa and other Romanos went to war to protect the colonies from themselves and their will to freedom, Mother told me of Uncle. He was a sensitive man, not known for ever having had a girlfriend. He enjoyed smoking cigarillos when he went to balls with his friends, and that, at a time men smoked tobacco leaves wrapped in fine, white, translucent rolling paper glued with saliva.

---

15. The Spanish Influenza pandemic of 1918 was so severe in Portugal that it is commonly known as "the Pneumonic". Without modern vaccines and treatments, the death rates of the epidemic were very high. Almost all Portuguese families lost loved family and friends because of it.

Over the years, Mother had developed a theory explaining why Uncle Romano was called an ass. It was not quite a theory. It was more of a syllogism which, in consequence, demystified werewolves and their covert nocturnal gatherings.

"Freedom, Matilde, is our most surprising and wildest inner wish, and therefore, it is the one which most imprisons us and the one which costs us the most," she said, when we started talking about Uncle because the son of our bailiff had just gone overseas to fight in the colonies.

At first, I thought we were talking about the looming war in Angola and the other colonies. There had been massacres of white settlers, and we, the Metropolis, needed to rush to save the poor souls who were being quartered with machetes throughout the farms of the hinterland. But no, her eyes were staring into the past, and freedom was not related to our lack of political democracy or the dawning war and impaled white farmers.

"Your Uncle was freed by war. It is strange when it is war that pacifies us. If he had returned, his war wouldn't have ended," she continued.

"How's that? What are you saying, Mother?"

"Your Uncle did not belong to that time or those people."

"Because they said he was a werewolf?"

"Hum," she assented, and kept on looking beyond the window panes of her study into an indistinct horizon. Who knows but that her eyes were not looking at a muddy trench where, so many years before, a Portuguese man in the prime of life had fallen with eyes dull with death.

"I never understood that, why people spoke such a nonsense of Uncle Romano."

"Because it wasn't nonsense."

There was no one like Mother for laconism, you know? If, at first, her vague words made me put an abrupt stop to our conversations and rush out through the door and away from her, life had meanwhile taken care of domesticating my impulses. When the war in the African colonies broke out, I had already gotten to a stage where I was fully aware that Mother inhabited a time of her own, one whose rhythm was not our own either. I had also learned meantime that time is not that speedy thing of our younger years. Time needs time, and we only get to the understanding of it when we stop fighting to outrun it. And that is why you usually beat the time you lend us.

"How come it was not a nonsense?" I persisted.

"Because it wasn't. Have you ever noticed, my Daughter, that werewolves were all men? And that everybody knew who was a werewolf?"

"Ah...," I knew at last. It had taken me half a century to know who Uncle Romano really was and to realise that my Mother was infinitely wiser than I had ever imagined her to be in those silences of hers. I understood distinctly, like someone who sees the simplest, clearest thing in the world, that Mother, who had spent her life surrounded by ghosts and other supernatural phenomena, had never believed in werewolves. "So that was a protection?" I asked in a whisper, without expecting any answer, and only because the question came out in a reflex that my lips did not trap in time.

Her assent was spoken in the silence in which she had entered so as to say the conversation was over. It was always like that. The final word was hers, a word spoken by retiring to her inner world of mute words.

And I? I understood only too well what it meant to be an ass. The interpretation of Mother's certainties and silences, my decades of existence in all the experiences I had lived, allowed me to, finally, grasp why my Uncle was that. And yes, I understood why Mother said freedom is the wildest wish of our innermost selves and why the rural folk, in their servitude, had chosen ass-werewolves to represent the liberty of those living on the margins.

My poor Uncle, what favour you did him in La Lys. For once you were life, and I cannot but thank you for that as well.

IV

For each time I lived, I died. Death was always a conspicuous presence; therefore the physicality of this body dying is, if not a comforting idea, at least one with which I have come to terms, and that is probably why I am still here. Death always had a way of reminding me I was alive. Now that I have little use for life, it hides behind the horizon. I know, in addition, that I will go on living after I no longer live. Mother made sure of telling me that after she died.

In the vault of the Boshoff of Nothing, in the cemetery of Ladeirinhas, I have already had the shelf between the Father and the Son cleared. It is the place Luísa of Nothing will inhabit after she sheds this wrinkled cocoon. Mother's coffin was put on the upper shelf, in front of those who enter and just beneath the crucified Christ hanging below the porthole that filters the dim light illuminating the souls and the still air of the sepulchre.

Neither could it be another way. She always lived in a space above us, not merely on the first floor of the house of Nothing,[16] where she resided as if levitating over us. Without doing anything for it, she always held the grand stage of our lives on which she walked like some great, temperamental diva. It could not have been any different in death. Therefore, the day they bury me in no ground in the vault, hers is the coffin you will see first. I will stay with mine to the right of the entrance, whereas our pasts are neatly put on dust-ridden shelves to the left.

I wonder whether you will feel the curiosity to come in? After all, that is no longer your business. It is an after-you, a land where we have gotten rid of you and where you do not live.

Maybe they threaten us with life there, the same way they threaten us with death here. Interesting to think of it.

---

16. The "first floor" in Portugal, as in many countries in Europe, is the floor above the ground floor. It is variously known as the "second floor" in other countries, including the United States.

"Come on, Má, eat. Why do you do this to us?" I heard these words, uttered a thousand times over, in a voice heavy with lost hope, with Father using Mother's pet name, Má. It was in reality his affectionate shortening of her name, Máxima, but ironic as it could be and was at those times, "má" is also the word for "mean."

And mean was what I thought she was for making us go through all that living hell. I would listen outside the door of Mother's room when Father went there with yet another tray of Engrácia's freshly prepared chicken soup. It was a rich, invigorating soup, garnished with the sharp yellow balls of immature eggs taken from the guts of dead egg-laying hens. Our hope was that the soup could put an end to Mother's unnatural fast.

Mother had what the people colloquially called "moons"; obscure phases during which she would remain in bed for days and days. She would not eat, and Father despaired at that, as had my grandmother Sabina, who was the one who looked after Mother before Manuel Tibério came along. Perhaps that had been the reason for my grandmother's demise so soon after marrying off her daughter. Weary of all the worries, she handed over to someone else the heavy burden of taking care of her daughter's strange life.

I remember hot tears rolling down my face each time I heard Father talking to Mother in the days when everything around the house was about Mother's condition. The "moon". I could not make any noise because Mother was resting. Father would arrive earlier from his chores to try to get her to eat. Grandfather would seek asylum in the cellar because he could not stand another of his daughter's crises. I could not run in the corridors after the cats of the house. Those were days of hell, and I asked the same question as Father: "Why do you do this to us?"

"Eat, Máxima, you'll see it tastes delicious. It's that wonderful soup made with the *pedreses*[17] that your father is so proud of raising. What's the matter with you?"

By this time Father already knew Mother did not have a doctor's

---

17. Plural form of Pedrês Portuguesa, a chicken breed native to Portugal.

illness. Given the incomprehensible nature of her condition, calling whatever it was that afflicted Mother a "moon" was indeed an appropriate word to name those periods of a causeless prostration. Their frequency was as irregular as her whims dictated but as predictable as any lunar cycle. It looked as if she took leave of life and moved to a suspended state. We never knew the reasons: Why would she give herself to such an ailment? Perhaps she needed a periodic rest from life.

Hence, if you think you took her, you are so wrong. She left the stage when she wished, through the ways which had been familiar to her all her life.

I cried in anger because Nothing entered a state of hibernation each time Mother had one of her "moons". I cried in anger because she did not care enough for me or for Father to protect us from those afflictions. Above all, I cried because I pitied Father. He did not deserve being a victim to something like that.

After leaving the tray in the room, from where it would come out untouched the next morning for as long as the condition lasted, Father put on his usual face to pretend that only a few seconds before he had not been with that distant woman and disheartened to the depths of his soul. He could be shattering inside but would not let me or my Grandfather witness his grief.

I helped play the charade. Hiding in the corner of the corridor leading to my bedroom, I would not let him see me. It would tear my heart out if ever he had to go through the humiliation of knowing that I knew of his broken, powerless begging of Mother to get up, eat and live a life as normal as any other woman's.

Apparently, Mother had inherited her "moons" from her grandmother, Argentina, who came from Porto de Mós to marry the firstborn heir of Nothing. Nevertheless, my great-grandmother's "moons" were not as eerily refined as Mother's. In fact, Grandfather Américo was not very keen on hearing comments about his mother's episodes that bordered on lunacy, because they would certainly tarnish the memories he kept of her. But Engrácia was always willing to tell me the stories surrounding my great-grandmother's absentmindedness, which were quite famous in Ladeirinhas, and I laughed a good laugh imagining a woman whose mind was perpetually up in the clouds.

There was a pool of water, framed by some weeping-willows and washing boards, in a shallow, wider part of the stream that ran at the bottom of Nothing. It was where the maids did our washing and their own. Once, when my great-grandmother had finished dying some lengths of fabric in big cauldrons over the fire, she took the newly dyed strips to the pool so the cold water would set the colours. By chance, it was on a fine day when a group of women was busy doing the washing. She took off her shoes, walked into the water and started washing the fabric, which quickly turned the water a rich blue.

"O, Mrs. Argentina, for pity's sake! Go wash those cloths somewhere else. You're soiling our water," they cried. She instantly apologised, grabbed the fabric, got out of the water and, doing as she had been asked, went somewhere else. To everyone's bewilderment, blue water started coming into the pool. Instead of having moved downstream, great-grandmother had gone upstream.

She did not do those things out of malice; it was simply in her nature to lose track of reality. And that she did, all the time.

There was another story about a day she had ridden on horseback to Vila Franca to run some errand. On her way back to Nothing, she dismounted and walked the rest of the way, leading the horse by the reins. A few boys, knowing her daydreaming ways, snuck behind her back and loosened the animal's harness, leaving her pulling the reins without a horse. She crossed Ladeirinhas looking every bit as ridiculous as could be and only realised the horse was gone when she got to Nothing.

She died, old in years, saying she had to take lunch to her son Josézinho, who was picking olives. The truth was that her son had drowned in a tub of fermenting must, thirty years before. It was June when she died, and olives are not ripe for picking until November. In old age she had totally lost her mind—not that she had much of it when she was young—and the single scariest thing that could befall my family was that any of us might die a bit insane as had grandmother Argentina.

Mother's alienation was different. While old Argentina had had a brood of children and kept herself busy from dawn to dusk dying cloths, kneading bread or killing and skinning rabbits, my Mother was estranged from my Father and spent her days alone, either in her study or in her bedroom.

When she was not too weary, she would come down to the dining room to eat supper with us. Otherwise, I had lunch in the kitchen with Engrácia and the help, and in the evening, dinner was shared between my Father, Grandfather and me in the dining room—which had been the living room when Nothing was named Candeia and before Argentina's father-in-law had had construction work done to enlarge the house.

On the very rare occasions Mother went out, she asked that her copper red mare be groomed and readied, and she vanished into the fields. No one ever found out where those mysterious outings took her, and I cannot say whether Father was curious enough to follow her. I suspect he respected her privacy but, out of pure precaution, he might have asked someone to check her whereabouts and make sure she would not get lost or fall down a ravine or a ditch. After all, he had also heard the stories of crazy Argentina.

In any case, I have never known anything about Mother's occasional disappearances.

I started to think she was beautiful after I realised she was different, back on the day we bid our farewell to Uncle Romano at the train station in Vila Franca. She was blonder than I, of a blond that never turned grey because it was already too light to lose colour. She was tall, just like all of us, slightly taller than I, slim and of lean flesh. Hers was an abundant, round bust, made more so given the stark contrast with her fine waist and overall thinness.

Her single most striking feature, however, was her colourless blue eyes. Never in the days of my life have I seen eyes which said more about someone's character than those. We are all blue-eyed in Nothing. Our eyes come in kaleidoscopic variations of blue, but hers were, of all eyes known in memory, the lightest, coldest and hardest. The black of her pupil stood in staggering antagonism with the watery, transparent blue of the iris. Its impact, tremendous.

You could never have seen yourself reflected in her eyes. They mirrored nothing that indicated what she was seeing. Besides, I think she did not even see you, because she was not in the least interested in you.

When I now think of her eyes, I think it possible she did not go out of the house much because light made her eyes hurt, just as it does mine, but whose discomfort I endure in the eagerness of seeing. She, on the other hand, was not that bothered if she did not see the world outside. She inhabited a world where sight was a sense of the mind and so was unhurt by the glare from which we always sought refuge behind the shade of our multiple large brimmed hats. Along the way, by one of those unexpected twists of fate, I discovered tinted glasses, which she never wore, and I started to see more clearly.

Yes, the bitter, cold severity of her gaze represented the exact measure of her stern personality and the unfathomable iciness of her imperturbable soul.

She was never one to hold me in her arms as Father used to do when he arrived home after a day's work. I would run to him, my arms open and a gummy smile of tender age losing its baby teeth, in the sweet anticipation of his warm embrace. I never saw her laugh or heard her sing as I used to hear Father. Nor did I ever hear from her sounds that were more surprised or heated or happier or sadder.

Hers was not a monotonous voice that rendered her speech boring or uninteresting. Inversely, it had a loftiness of nothing, capable of suspending us in the attention devoted to whatever she had to say, which was invariably scarce in quantity and duration. I believe we were surprised each time we heard her voice and, consequently, we were utterly impressed by her on those rare occasions we were presented with the sound of her voice.

Had she made the world her stage instead of confining herself to the study and her bedroom in Nothing, she might have been an Eva Péron. Clad in sober elegance, she favoured cosmopolitan accessories so unlike the rural atmosphere of Nothing. From Lisbon she would have precious Flanders lace brought so *Dona* Ifigénia could make her the most fashionable dresses. Dressed thus, she resembled a translucent, light fairy, or so my mind thought. She was never truly ours.

My relationship with her went through several phases – rough patches, I should perhaps call them.

Little do I remember of her in my early childhood. I remember instead the soft, warm bosom of Engrácia and her smell of kitchen and toasted oatmeal porridge. Then I remember my secret crying and asking why Mother had to be so strange and so unbearable.

When I was around fourteen or fifteen, I would take the horse Grandfather had offered me and I stormed out each time she was under one of her peculiar "moons". It was then I discovered the lake of still waters where the course of the Rio Grande ebbed before meeting the Tagus a bit further down the stream.

It was a wonderful place of peace and quiet. Under the shade of the oaks, the water reflected the dim rays of sun that managed to penetrate the thick foliage. Not mirroring the turquoise of the sky, the water instead took on the murky brown of its muddy bed, shadowed by the trees around the lake. I cherished that place for the healthy tranquility it provided me, away from the oppressive, silence in which Nothing was immersed in the days Mother was going through a crisis.

The lake was, however, a treacherous one. Beneath the apparent surface stillness, the Rio Grande rushed in its urgency to reach the Tagus. And the deceptively still, dense placidity of the water closer to the banks was said to tire even the most experienced of swimmers.

When she found out I enjoyed going to the lake, Mother summoned me to her room and told me she did not want me near the lake again. It would be up to Engrácia to explain the reason for the prohibition, which, in all honesty, I never obeyed. Apparently, Mother was afraid I might enter that lying water which had killed before. People had drowned there, entangled in submersed tree trunks and branches. Others had perished in rescuing attempts, when the water that was so still on the surface became heavy and pulled swimmers down to the waiting depths. Misfortunes all, which the people liked to recount over and over again. Episodes of mourning that alleviated the sameness of days.

Later, when Father was dying, was when my relationship with her went through its roughest patch. I scolded her. I blamed her for not having made Father happy. I went as far as calling her a lunatic. Never did I manage to treat her with the familiarity I used in my interactions with Father. To me she was always a formal Someone I had to address with deference. And, on seeing Father saying goodbye to life, I thought I would be incapable of ever dealing with her dead soul confined in a house that, by force of circumstances, I was henceforth bound to carry on my shoulders as the sole heir of Nothing.

I despised her. I forgot I had decided to love her when she gave me the shelf in her bookcase. By then I had nothing but Nothing, and it frustrated me to realise that, ironically, what was going to be left of us as a family was that woman with whom it had always been so difficult to communicate. My immortal Father was going away, leaving me alone with Mother, and I was at a total loss to manage my relationship with her. The paradox was incomprehensible to my heart. The whole thing shook me to the core.

For a long time afterwards, all I could muster for her were bristly responses, my anger at her masked under a cloak of indifference. More than once I heard myself telling her to her face I was not going to tolerate her "moons" and that I had every intention of dispatching her to an asylum if she did not cure herself.

Those were horrible times of an unbridled rage that may have given you enormous pleasure to watch. But you know it was all out of pain and loss, do you not? Of course, you know. After all, you were always there for the losses.

She, on the other hand, remained unperturbed by my furies, which only added to my ire, for I thought her lack of emotion was her way of mocking my distressed spirit.

Then came calm. I must have wakened one day to the recognition that the mother Providence had paired me with was that woman, so all my crying and yelling, indifference, and attempts at escaping from her were pointless. My Mother was that person, and that was it.

I accepted her at long last, and that brought the peace I had been lacking all my life. Because I never heard Father upset with her, not even when he was asking her to eat or why did she treat us thus, I assume he had also accepted her, out of his deep love for her.

I understand, my God, how I understand, how he must have loved her, beyond all possible human comprehension. It was not only having fallen in love and marrying her in his youth, a time when we can do everything and want everything. It was also having endured the emotional burden of loving her in all that was strange about her: the whispers coming from her bedroom in the wee hours; the seamstress who was audible only to her and that we attributed to some electric phenomenon occurring in the corner of her study; the "moons"; the physical and emotional distancing of someone who never gave herself to us. He bore it all.

I do not believe it was out of stoicism. It was out of love.

But you have no idea what that is and hence my pitying you.

V

In the summer of 1930, I was nineteen and still grieving Grandfather Américo's death. It had taken us by surprise in February, just when we were sighing with relief that the winter was almost over and he would be with us another year.

Of late, he had been feeling the wintry season to be hard to withstand. He started wearing layer upon layer of disconnected pieces of clothing: pullovers on top of jackets over shirts, and still the cold got to his bones. He no longer tended the chickens he was so proud of. He instead spent his days by the fireplace in the kitchen. The occasional sunny days found him sitting, sheltered from the chilly breezes, by the west wall of the house. He frequently caught colds and convalescence became his daily life. Then the season changed and he was back to his former self until the next winter, which would, invariably, be harder to bear than the previous one.

That year he had contracted pneumonia. He only left the house to make the journey to the cemetery to join the other Boshoff of Nothing. Father lost a father and I lost a man who had always been there for me, more even than my own Father, whose colossal affairs — managing the plentiful acres in Nothing, the wine, the lands, the olive-press, the whole lot — kept him far too busy to mind my upbringing as he wished he could.

Probably more than anyone else, Father had more than enough reasons to mourn Grandfather. They loved each other as though the same blood ran in their veins. They had shared twenty-one years of Nothing and of life together. Most of all, they had shared the difficult task of loving my Mother and holding her to life.

As for me, it was Grandfather who taught me to predict the weather.

"Mm... the weather is changed, Lizzie", he would say, looking authoritatively at the skies and sensing the change in the smell and density of the air. He would always be right: Then came rain or heat or wind.

"It's blowing from under," he would say, referring to strange winds blowing north from Africa, a bad sign in a place where winds were supposed to sweep south and east from northern or western latitudes. That kind of wind meant heavy rainfall that could seep through the fissures of doors and windows. "Yup! It's blowing from under," he would say, the certainty of confirmation in his voice after the storm had set in.

He would stand at the kitchen door, facing the porch, hands behind his back. And there he stayed, joyfully contemplating the storm, happy that his prediction had materialised.

He also taught me not to be afraid of thunder when poor Engrácia knelt praying to Saint Barbara to ward off the storm that she said soured the milk.

And it was Grandfather who taught me the times of the earth: the right times to prune, to sow, to sulphurise the grapevines, to weed, to mow, to harvest. I loved going out with him to the olive groves in October to inspect the olives and check whether they would soon be ripe for reaping. The first to be harvested we would put in a large amphora-like jar and leave them to marinate in an aromatic, salty seasoning of lemon wedges, garlic, oregano and *erva-azeitoneira*,[18] a special herb that grows wild near olive trees and whose only use I take to be that of curing olives. So the olives could be infused with the flavours, we would cut them top to bottom, a process which, invariably, blackened our fingers. Then we put the sliced olives in the marinade and changed the water of the marinade once a week for at least a month, until they were ready to eat.

The next time Grandfather and I went to the groves would already be harvest season. The olives would be beaten off the trees with long, flexible sticks. The women would gather the black olives from where they had fallen. The men would take them to the rank-smelling press, from whence, paradoxically, poured this velvety, golden-green liquid that made our roasted cod come alive. And was drizzled over our boiled potatoes, which I mashed on my plate so as to better mix

---

18. *Erva-azeitoneira* is an herb that grows wild in Mediterranean areas and, in particular, near olive groves. With a flavour that could be described as akin to that of thyme, in Portugal it is mostly used to season cured olives.

them with the olive oil. A number of gaibéus[19] from the Beiras would show up to help us with the task of collecting our precious olives. Forsaken people known for their large families and extreme poverty, they would arrive in a flock, and as a flock they slept in the barn or the cellar. After the harvesting was done, they would go back to the far, indistinct horizon from where they had come, and there they remained until the next year. It was a complete mystery to me how they guessed it was time to pick the olives and arrived at our gates every year like clockwork.

There was one particular year when, out of absolute rarity, Mother decided to go to the olive groves and see how the harvesting was going. She showed up at around dinner time, which back then corresponded to lunch. Because it was a November of glorious weather, she came holding a lace umbrella aloft, protecting herself from the sun. There, in the midst of all those people, I thought I had never seen anything or anyone more beautiful. I was sharing my day with the workers and was eating some bread with thick red chorizo slices.[20] I smiled and looked at her, and she seemed to smile back at me.

She went her way, and after a few moments we heard someone screaming, "Help! The Lady is unwell!" I stood up, tossing the basket containing my meal, and ran like crazy through the grove.

When I got to Mother, she was unconscious, and I feared the worst. We took her home, where gradually she came to. She had no recollection of anything other than having felt like going for a walk to enjoy such a lovely day. We told her she had gone to the olive grove and she stared at us as if we were saying the most absurd thing. How was that possible? She had no memory of having left the house. She swore she had not yet made up her mind about whether to go out or not.

---

19. Colloquialism to designate the poor people from the Northern provinces of Portugal, or Beiras, who would often come looking for seasonal work on the farms of more southerly provinces, particularly during the months of olive harvesting in November and December.

20. Chorizo is the Spanish word for *chouriço*, a smoked cured sausage typical of Mediterranean countries, made red by paprika used to season the meat.

We did not insist. She put on her most nonchalant attitude, as if saying we could tell her anything we wanted, she would not believe us, and it was perfectly alright. We did not know what had really happened that day, so we attributed the incident to her peculiar ways. But later in the evening, Grandfather said he remembered a similar episode when she was about eight. Moments before she was found unconscious, she had been seen looking like she was floating in the company of angels with exactly the expression I had seen earlier when in the grove I thought she had smiled at me and was the most beauteous creature on Earth.

After Grandfather died, it was strange to be left in a world where I had only my parents. Every single day I would miss riding out in the vineyards with Father and Grandfather, or the three of us going to see the latest calf to have been born. I missed our sitting at the table for supper and talking about the events of the day. I found it awkward to eat alone with Father. It was as though we engaged in conversation only to push aside any memories of Grandfather and mask that emptiness which was so filled with his presence. I missed our being three and I felt an enormous and painful mutilation at what was the first, irreversible loss of my life.

The lake on the Rio Grande at the far end of Nothing opposite the Salgueirinha farm, which was also ours, was where I sought refuge in those days of mourning. It was the lake of dangerous still waters, where I had kept going in bold defiance of Mother's orders.

And it was there I met him for the first time.

I heard the soft thuds of the horse's hooves even before I saw him. I was sitting with my back leaning against the rough trunk of an oak tree, contemplating the tranquil water and the fallen, golden leaves of the oaks which floated, unsinkable, on the surface. I was indulging in grief when horse and rider disrupted my thoughts.

He was the son of the new judge of Vila Franca, the town by the mighty Tagus closest to Nothing. He was unacquainted with the region, so was scouting the area. He apologised in case he was trespassing. His speech was courteous and polished. He must have studied at some fancy school, not with a Mademoiselle Mirabelle who had since left for having taught me everything she knew.

I felt illiterate and reduced to nothing, I, who was used to being the Daughter of Manel of Nothing. He dismounted and I felt less diminished in the comparison. He was only a boy turning into a man, just as I was a girl turning into a woman.

He was probably a mere two or three years my senior. He had recently come back from college, in Coimbra, and was spending his holidays with his parents in Vila Franca. He told me more about himself than I told him of me.

Yes, he should feel free to come there whenever he wanted. This was Nothing, and if he continued his journey up the trail under the trees, he would get to the yard of the farm.

"Uh, Nothing! I've heard that name," he exclaimed, smiling.

And I said, yes, it was possible he had heard of us because there might not be so many Nothings around.

He mounted again and, as he was about to turn away, he said his name was António.

"Luísa."

The following day at the same hour we met by the lake. I did not give a thought to whether anyone might get suspicious of this, my new habit of unexplained absences. The chance of coming across that horseman was far too alluring for a heart which was blossoming to men other than the patriarchs of Nothing.

I was about to give up when he reappeared. I blushed at the thought that he might guess I was there on purpose. Lies had never been natural in my personality, and I could be easily exposed as a liar. In any case, guessing my intents or not, he played the ignorant gentleman. It was all one lucky coincidence that he had felt like going for a ride in the neighbourhood and I had sought the cool shade of the oaks on that stifling August day. The air was filled with the incessant hum of bees and dragonflies that drank on the surface of the lake but, apart from that, summer there was as silent and dormant as the darkish, still water.

He dismounted again. He grabbed a pebble and threw it to the water so that it skipped its way to the middle of the lake.

I told him I had learnt that trick from my Grandfather and

showed him.

I laughed a lot that afternoon. The laughter I had been incapable of since Grandfather died. It was as if sadness had abandoned me. Or never existed. Suddenly it seemed the valley of darkness, about which I had been taught in Sunday School, had come to an end. Little did I know back then what a valley of darkness truly was.

When he left, we promised to meet there again the following day.

That night I whispered his name a thousand times whilst I turned over and over in my bed made with the cool linen sheets we used in summer. I found it difficult to fall asleep; I had never been in a state of such anxiety before.

António. António. António. He was called António. These were the foolish feelings of someone abruptly waking from childhood.

It was then I started writing diaries. One day I went to the grocery in Ladeirinhas and bought a notebook and green silk paper. I lined the notebook with the silk paper and filled it with António.

Of course there was no fooling Engrácia. It took her only a blink of an eye to suspect there was something peculiar going on.

"O my, isn't she distracted, this Child?" she cooed, the time she caught me daydreaming and burning the rice pudding I was stirring over the stove. Startled, I pulled myself together and went back to stirring the pudding.

Our meetings became frequent, and one day he asked from me a kiss. I told him no, that I was embarrassed. I remembered what I had heard about Aunt Margarida, and the loneliness of my growing up made me particularly ignorant. He did not insist.

The next day he arrived at the front gate of Nothing. An older man accompanied him. They looked like two centaurs coming from some unexpected nothing. I sent for Father so he could welcome the two gentlemen.

"Well, Mr. Tibério, it seems these two have become quite the friends", the older man told my Father after having introduced himself as the father of the younger man and being taken to the living-room, where Father poured him a Port in a crystal goblet.

In my scared bewilderment I looked at Father, trying to figure out his reaction. My thoughts ran wild, and my heart was pounding. Father, obviously, was in shock; surprise eclipsed all words he could have said. There was a judge telling him their children were friends, or better, more than friends, whatever that was.

"Indeed, Mr. Tibério," the judge continued, "I am a man of rectitude, who honours and respects the daughters of other men as if they were my own. With your permission, I would like to ask you whether my son might be allowed to visit your daughter on Sundays after the ten o'clock Mass."

Father looked at me, trying to conceal the perplexity that was still visible in his eyes at the unusual situation, and answered.

"If it is of my Luísa's wish, you have my permission."

"So, Miss Luísa," the judge said, turning his eyes towards me, "what do you say? Do you consent to my António calling on you?"

I nodded. Father was not the only one to have been caught by surprise. I was mortified with embarrassment. Maybe that was what courtship was. What an awkward situation! My cheeks were so hot they were on the verge of exploding. All I wished was for those moments to be over as soon as possible. I could not stop staring at the floor — the floor I wished could engulf me and my shame of being there. I wanted to disappear. And I wanted everyone else to disappear as well.

When António and his father went away, Father gave me the expected third degree.

Where had I met him? Why had I not told him anything? Above all, what had already happened?

I put his fears to rest and told him António and I had only talked and nothing else.

I felt him start to relax. After all, I was becoming a young lady and, sooner or later, something like this was bound to happen.

There, there, nothing had happened and that was the most important thing. The judge seemed a man of character and, by Jove, he was a judge and his son was a Coimbra graduate. It could be worse.

I had not had the many suitors Mother had. Neither was I like her, who in her prime loved to stage an appearance, all dressed up and beautiful, at the balls and festivities of the vicinities, thus cementing her fame as inaccessible beauty queen who revelled in playing hard to get. I had a more down-to-earth nature. My days were spent out in the fields under a hot sun that tanned my alabaster skin—the complexion of a true child of Nothing. I dressed in work skirts and riding boots, and the only jewellery I never parted with were the gold ruby-studded earrings which had belonged to grandmother Sabina and Grandfather had given me on the day of my Solemn Communion.

Never had I thought about boys, and I had never been to the balls in Ladeirinhas because there was always plenty to keep me busy at Nothing. Sometimes I would accompany Father and Grandfather to Vila Franca to see the running of the bulls down the streets of the town and into the arena, or I would go with the family to Ladeirinhas on festival days to see the Procession as it passed in front of the churchyard. I took enjoyment in those special outings. Compared to Mother I must have seemed a housemaid.

The following Sunday I realised all eyes were on me at Mass. No sooner had Father told her about the visit from the judge and his son, than Mother sent for me. She told me that from now on I had to rise to the occasion: I was now a promised Lady. Suddenly I felt I had lost control of my life and wondered if I wanted to be a promised Lady, whatever that was. Why could I not just meet António by the lake, if we were doing nothing wrong?

In only a few days, *Dona* Ifigénia had to make me a dress like the ones Mother wore, fluid and with a low waistline which lent height and slimness to a woman's frame. Luckily, as Mother emphasized, so as to make me see how graceless I was for not already having a collection of lovely dresses, there were lengths of crêpe Georgette remaining from the making of her own dresses that could be used. But it was imperative that other nice fabrics be brought from Lisbon so I could be fitted with a more suitable wardrobe now that I had come of age. I considered the whole a tiresome affair.

Up until then, it had been Engrácia and another maid who made my cotton skirts and cambric blouses. Now I was supposed to stand still while *Dona* Ifigénia took my measurements and stuck pins to mark the hemline of the dresses. And, as if all that were not enough,

I was made to wear some beige, kid leather gloves, which made me lose all my tactile senses, and high heels. As a sign that I had reached a bridal age, Mother had opened a drawer of the walnut commode and took out a lace mantilla which had once belonged to her mother, and her grandmother before, and her great-grandmother before them all, and that, henceforward, would belong to me.

All dolled up, there I went with the family of Nothing to attend Mass in Ladeirinhas. Even the Priest came to greet me after he officiated the rite. But not in his usual manner. Suddenly, it was as though he was not greeting Luísa, the daughter of Manel of Nothing, but Matilde, the daughter of Máxima, a Matilde so like her mother in the way she dressed and looked.

Quite aware of the transformation my clothes seemed to bring to the way people were now looking at me, I watched in amazement as the priest greeted me with the same deference he had always offered up to my mother.

That was a strange thing, for I was not known to be as peculiar as she was. I was the Daughter of Manel of Nothing and she was the Lady. It was difficult for those people to reconcile my new image with the person I really was. That might have been the major reason I was greeted with a collective gaze of speechless awe when I walked into the church and headed to the front row of seats where the owners of Nothing had sat throughout the ages to hear Mass.

When we arrived back at Nothing, António was already there, waiting for us, as agreed. He was still on horseback, sitting tall in the saddle with only his felt hat providing some shade from the sun of high morning. It was only when he saw us start to get down from the landau that he dismounted. He shook Father's hand, held his hat against his chest in a sign of respect, and helped the ladies.

As convention dictated, or so I thought, my parents excused themselves by reason of being tired from having been to Mass, retired into the back of the house, leaving us alone in the sitting room where we were properly guarded by Engrácia.

Never had I seen her as stiffly composed as when she was sitting in front of us, her back firmly planted against the chair's round back.

She was respect incarnate.

A maid came in, carrying a tray with three glasses for a sweet refreshment made of water and currant syrup.

After she left the room, the silence was deafening. The clock's pendulum marked the time of suspended nothing, and I could count second after second of slow, dragging nothingness.

My brain was about to explode. I felt like asking António, what kind of a charade was this? Why had he told me nothing about speaking to my Father? Why had he not given me a hint of his intentions? Moreover, if this was dating, I would have nothing of it. In that painfully long moment of renewed awkwardness, it did not seem I was in front of the joyous man-boy I had met by the lake and who had asked me for a kiss.

He was the one who started the conversation. I was too mad, too uncomfortable in that ridiculous dress and stupid gloves to even look at him, let alone speak to him.

"You look very lovely today, Miss Luísa."

From my lowered face I could see Engrácia looking askance at us; her hands crossed over her lap and solemn importance puffing up her chest.

"Thank you," I replied, out of courteous obligation.

"It seems today is the day of Saint Hyacinth. Do you happen to know anything about him?" António asked, pointing to the fact that it was August 17.

The situation was getting insufferable. How was I to know about Saint Hyacinth? And what did I care? I had never paid much attention to the teachings at Sunday School, and I only attended Mass because we were supposed to go to church on Sunday. Was there nothing more interesting for him to ask? We had talked freely about so many things when we were by the lake and now all he was doing was wasting hollow words.

No. I did not want any of that. Definitely not. I thought I liked António and, convinced that we could spend more time together, I had acquiesced to his father's proposal that he should visit me. But this had never been in my plans. I wished the time of the pointless interview could run fast so he would leave. After that, I would find a way to tell Father I had made a mistake. I did not want to receive visits from the judge's son. Father would understand, and I would be left alone.

I managed to utter a few insipid words and sighed with relief when Engrácia stood up from her chair to let us know time was up. Never had I blessed that woman more than then.

He said goodbye to me at the bottom of the outer stairs that led to the house of Nothing. He held my hand delicately so as to kiss it for courtesy's sake and, on doing so, he let me feel he was leaving something akin to paper in my kid-skin-lined palm.

I closed my hand as he winked at me. Flushed, I climbed the steps to the balcony in front of the main door where Engrácia was, all the while praying she had noticed neither the piece of paper being put in my hand nor the wink.

"Tomorrow at the lake."

It was the first and only time ever I saw his handwriting.

VI

When I got to the lake he was already there. I was mad with fury, and all I could think about was the number of things I wanted to throw at him. My self-confidence was also back now that I was wearing the clothes I was used to wearing. Myriad words were boiling in my mind. They were about to burst as I let loose my rage at him. He anticipated my acidic mood long before I could explode and started to laugh.

"You have such lovely colours when you are mad, you know."

"Don't make fun of me. It doesn't suit you," I replied sharply.

"Do forgive me. It's no mockery, nor could I speak ill to such a beautiful lady who makes my heart ache so much."

"Don't be insolent! If I ached your heart, you would take pity on me and not make me go through this week of ridiculousness."

"When I couldn't even get half a kiss from you, I had no alternative but to circumvent the situation and ask your father's permission to court you."

I blushed.

Suddenly, I felt my rage dissolve, and my blood flowed freely to my heart as it had in the days when I saw him by the lake and we threw pebbles that ricocheted on the water's surface and talked, oblivious of either time or constraints — silly words in even sillier conversations.

Gently, he came to me and took my hand. It was the first time I had felt his skin; the first time I had felt the skin of a man of whom I was neither daughter nor granddaughter.

"You know," he whispered, "I also don't know who Saint Hyacinth was and haven't got the slightest interest in knowing."

I smiled and he, in return. In the awkwardness of the moment, I lowered my head, which he gently lifted by tucking his finger under my chin so I could face him.

"I'm interested in you."

His voice was not more than a murmur as his lips faintly touched mine. I saw his eyes so close I could see myself reflected in the black-streaked, grey irises. I did not see anything else, because of a sudden all my senses became one. I was capable only of feeling: the warmth, the wet, our breath.

I could feel a velvety wave of warmth coming through from underneath his shirt. He wrapped his arms around me and I thought my knees would fail me. It was as though I was not me anymore because I had never felt before. The neutrality of me, of my body, ended there.

When we parted from that kiss, we were a you of us and no longer a you of them. The formality of speech we had maintained was gone, and I knew that man would wed me.

Of this you know nothing. You have no idea what it is to become whole through the other. And you do not know life is skin of warm velvet: warmth — the only thing which distinguishes us from death.

After that, we endured the discomfort of another Sunday's courtship filled with empty conversation and Engrácia's stiff watching. Then we furtively escaped to our hideaway at the lake. Anxious, we determined he would ask for my hand the following Sunday. I smiled at the thought of Father going through the second shock in the space of a fortnight.

And so it was.

The next Sunday, when António was waiting for us to arrive from church, he was accompanied by his father.

My Father realised instantly that something was about to happen. This time the judge had lost the assertiveness of the first time he had been to our house. His speech was tentative; he was treading on foreign ground. After all, he was not the only one to have been caught by surprise.

"Imagine, Mr. Tibério," he eventually began, after having been invited to come into the living room. "It seems these two want to make us family. I know this is all too sudden, but my son assures me this has nothing to do with second intentions. O no, not in the least." He carried on, trying his best to assure my Father that my honour was intact, which, in those days, was the single reason that justified a hasty marriage. "He is so smitten by Luísa he doesn't mean . . . "

"Matilde. My daughter is called Matilde."

The interruption was my Mother's. She had arrived from Mass with us as usual but, having seen the judge, she had not withdrawn to her rooms. She instead had walked us into the room, more as gracious host than out of genuine interest.

In a split second we all turned our faces to her. Her voice of determined composure, along with her icy presence, trapped time for a moment. The pendulum of the clock stopped.

"Yes, I am Luísa Matilde."

I rushed to explain before the bewilderment of those present became even more disorienting: Father's, because of the imminent proposal; and António's and the judge's, because of the confusion regarding my name. To disencumber the moment, I entangled myself into Luísa and Matilde without feeling any more Matilde for that matter. It was Luísa who was in love.

"O right, Miss Luísa Matilde," the judge said, his embarrassment palpable, as if the problem of my wrongly pronounced name was due to his inexcusable ignorance.

"I was saying that my son is so truly enamored by your daughter that it is my solemn duty to ask you whether you grant us the honour of her marrying him."

António's abundant virtues were then listed and followed by the promise that an office was being set for him in Vila Franca so he could start his career as a lawyer and provide for a family and all the expected etceteras demanded of such an occasion.

Father listened to everything in silence.

When the praise for his proposing son-in-law ended, he just said, as two Sundays before, that it was up for me to decide and that if this was to my liking then he had nothing to object.

My heart raced with joy. I had never been as happy as in at that moment. I was going to marry António and that made me the luckiest, most fortunate creature on Earth.

I could have died then so I would die in contentment—in the utmost bliss, devoid of shadows like yours, untainted by regrets or sorrow.

Happiness in its purest state. I did not die, of course, but that is the instant I keep as a comparison to all other joyful moments I might have had until then and that I would ever experience in the future. That particular moment brought me the zenith of multiplied happiness and, if I felt that, I can say my life was unlike many, for I really knew what it is like to be happy when one is happy. I seized that instant with both hands. I was aware of it, and that consciousness is what differentiates those who genuinely live and know what happiness feels like from those who merely spend time in this life.

It was agreed that we would wait until the banns were called, and the wedding would take place after vintage, a period of intense labour at the farm.

In my daydreaming I imagined António would love Nothing and that we — he, Father and I — would go for walks in the vineyards as Father and I used to when Grandfather was alive.

Again, *Dona* Ifigénia was called in, to receive the order for my wedding dress and to be told she could hire an assistant to help her with the job. As always when there was a wedding at Nothing, no expense was spared for the celebration that marked the forging of a new generation to perpetuate the immortal legacy of Nothing.

My turn had come. I was the new, promise-filled link in that ancient chain. From me onwards, Nothing would go on living.

Still baffled by the unexpected events of recent days, Father was nonetheless in a joyous disposition. Mother was not moody as she sometimes was, and it was she who had *Dona* Ifigénia sent for and who stipulated how my dress should be made and how the chapel would be decorated. She wanted carmine leaves of harvested vines and basketfuls of grapes and early pomegranates which were ready to be picked in September in the orchard of Empena Quente,[21] where fruits always ripened earlier.

Those were exciting times loaded with potential, when work seemed effortless and light. The hope of days to come was the energy

---

21. Literally: Warm Slope.

flowing in our veins and, wherever we looked, all were good omens for a blissful eternity.

On account of my multiple chores imposed by vintage and planning a wedding, I rarely met António by the lake. Besides, he was also busy setting up a first-floor office on the street to the railway station in Vila Franca. He wanted to get married and settled into business.

Some time passed after the Sunday of the proposal before there was another Sunday when, through smiles and half words so Engrácia could not understand anything, we arranged to meet by the lake the following Friday.

He was already there, as I suspected he would be.

September was hot in its languid rivers and dry sources waiting for the stormy rains of October. The lake, with its quiet placidity, created a relaxing environment. I know not whether it was the heat or the peacefulness of the place, but the truth is there was no need for speech. In contrast to the heavy, uncomfortable silences of Sundays closely watched over by Engrácia, this was a silence of many words.

He came near me, and I longed with my every fiber that he kiss me.

Do you know what kind of a feeling it is, when you are sure that the thing you want the most is going to happen?

That was exactly how I felt when his lips spoke to me a language of words that outshone the ones I so much loved to speak.

Round. I would describe that kiss as round, for all that round means of full. Now that I already knew how to kiss, I gave myself to him, no longer pervaded by a mixed feeling of discovery and rationalisation of the act, but out of pleasure.

He felt it too.

When I came to, my eyes slowly opened and I saw light meandering through the dark green canopy of the oaks over my head. He had laid me on the ground amongst the fallen leaves and his hands had scouted the cartography of my body. I was neither scared nor ashamed. Neither was I nervous when I felt he was a man. I rocked myself in us and closed my eyes again. Because I longed for him, I let him make of me the woman I would henceforth be, in our disheveled clothes that got in the way without getting in the way, for nothing else matters and all is allowed.

When it was all over I was left in a semi-dream, albeit awake, suffused by the surrounding heat and filled with profound peace. I stared at him and saw him as for the first time. My eyes set on the soft skin between his neck and shoulder, and I could see it pulse with the life of youth. I pulled near and pressed my lips softly against that spot. Never would I forget that touch.

He had straight, brown hair parted to his right. His lips were fine and very expressive when he smiled. However, it was his gaze, so different from us from Nothing, that most captivated me. It was possible to read his eyes. I was reminded of Uncle Romano's eyes, which were so like my Father's eyes, too.

Then he turned onto his back and crossed his arms behind his head. His eyes contemplated the distance above and there was no sound of words. I leaned my face against his body and we stayed there in that talking silence.

As we were betrothed, and our parents had agreed on the marriage, António was now free to join us for Sunday Mass instead of having to wait for us like a convict at the gates of Nothing. Even Engrácia's vigilance could be slackened, which meant following a few steps behind us when we walked along the azalea alley of the garden of Nothing.

After the coming together by the lake, the Sunday that followed was tedious, notwithstanding the walk in the garden and his staying for the one o'clock dinner. We could hardly wait for another of our escapes.

In our now standard dissimulated gestures and half-muttered words, we managed to arrange to meet on the morrow at the lake by the cool of day, which in Nothing corresponded to the time when plants were watered and the herds were gathered before sundown.

VII

I left early in the morning to check the *diagalves*[22] vines whose vintage had started the week before and whose grapes were crushed in the small wine cellar of Outeirinho,[23] one of our adjacent properties.

Father was busy in the big cellar, receiving the tubs of *trincadeira*[24] which made the red wine for which Nothing was renowned and weighing the unfermented grape juice, the must, with a thermometer to verify the alcoholic degree[25] of the wine to be. The voices of the vintagers filled the air of Nothing. To me, that was the best time of year: The farm was alive and bustling with the sound of work.

I loved to hear Father and Grandfather talking about the results of the weighing of the must.

"This year, we're having 13 degrees from the vineyard at Foro. Not bad, but last year it was 13.5 degrees. Now, good, really good, my father, was that year when we got 14 degrees out of it. And no sugar added, as those crooks do."

This was the kind of conversation my Father had during vintage with my Grandfather, whom he called father.

From hearing them, I learnt there were unscrupulous people who tinkered with the alcoholic degree of must by adding sugar to the grapes when they were being crushed. Obviously, the wine thus obtained was only good for gullible townsfolk who knew nothing about wine. At Nothing we were serious about winemaking and would never soil our name by having less than premium wines.

I was particularly fond of *diagalves*, which produced a very

---

22. Variety of Portuguese white wine grape known for its sweetness.

23. Pronounced O-tay-ree´-ñoo. The literal meaning of Outeirinho is small hill.

24. Variety of grape used in the production of full-bodied red wines.

25. In Portugal, the volume of alcohol in wine is commonly measured in degrees Gay-Lussac. The higher the degrees, the more alcoholic the wine. In the old days, rural people considered a higher degree an indicator of the quality of the wine. Wines with higher degree were also sold at higher prices.

perfumed white wine, and was therefore much committed to tending that particular vineyard. We also owned a vineyard, Cruz, for table grapes, notably Dona Maria, a white variety of long, fleshy, firm grapes, which I absolutely loved, and delicious *moscatel*.[26]

That day, I went through my chores in the sweet anticipation of the coming of late afternoon. I ate from the thick slices of cod roasted under the deep turquoise skies that the workers who were vintaging at Outeirinho wanted to share with me.

I then went by the big cellar to check on Father and the progress of the crushing of the grapes and was about to head to Cruz to pick some *Dona Maria* that Engrácia had asked me to bring home when I heard the bells at the chapel of Nothing sounding the tocsin.

I turned my horse around and made for the house. The bell ringing in such despair could only mean fire. By late summer it was customary to clear the margins of streams and rivers of the bush that had grown wildly. It was a precautionary measure, so that when the first rains fell, the waters could run free. All vegetable waste was burned, and I assumed that somewhere a fire had spread out of control.

When I got to the courtyard of the big house of Nothing, I was met with the frenzy of distress.

"Miss Luísa, *Paizinho*[27] is gone with the men," someone shouted, out of breath, "There's a drowned man in the lake."

Hastening the gallop, I headed for the lake, my heart pounding in fear of what might be.

There was a wet, still body on the ground under the shade of the oaks. Father was bending over it, the air heavy with silence.

It was António, lying bluish and cold.

A corpse is a hideous thing; the expression no longer there. In Mother's novels I read about the serene aspect of dead people: their diaphanous, asleep-like look. António resembled more the horrendous agonising Christ, contorted with pain, at the altar in Ladeirinhas, his face disjointed and lacerated. Thus was António.

---

26. Muscat variety of wine and table grape, much appreciated in Portugal.

27. A term of endearment and respect, meaning, "your father."

Slightly open, purple lips let us see the dark emptiness inside his mouth. His eyelids were fixed midway down his eyes, showing an iris of vitreous nothing.

Disgust came over me, and I chastised myself for the nausea of the instant when I saw him in that grimace of ugliness which would remain with him forever and ever more.

I accursed you for the first time, as if, from within me, my hatred were blood and bile.

Only one thing had I wanted in life, one alone, and it had just been stolen from me with brusque, lacerating violence. I choked back my scream because, had I unleashed it, I would have died, my lungs as drowned as António's.

He had arrived early for our get together and while waiting for me sought refuge from the stifling heat in the coolness of that deceitfully still water. Alas, he was a foreigner who knew nothing of the perils lurking in the lake. Poor soul. Now he was another casualty added to the list of people killed by those dead and deadly waters.

I urged someone to go, silence the bell and have it toll instead.

Father's speechlessness spoke loudly. He wanted to tell me what he knew not how to tell me. I believe a piece of his soul died on seeing me in the desolation caused by António's death.

Nobody asked what he had been doing there at that time. They knew he had been there on account of me. And I sensed Father must be thinking about Aunt Margarida who had also perished because love had to be furtive. António had died because of the tongues of people, because of scandals and the many things we invent to thwart them before they burst into the plain sight of everyone.

Nothing stood still.

When we emerged from the steep footpath leading to the yard in front of the houses of Nothing, the silence and silent faces were fixed on me and on António's limp body lying across the back of his horse. He had looked so imposing when I saw him come from behind the trees that first day by the lake. And so majestic astride the horse when he waited for us at the gates of Nothing. Now he was nothing but a lifeless bundle. I needed to conjure all my strength to shut my heart to the pain inflicted by the sight: António's corpse, soaking and inglorious, alone before the public gaze which takes pity on death. I felt ashamed for him and for what he might have felt had he known he resembled a broken, humiliated Hector at the gates of Troy.

There came the Masters of Nothing carrying a dead man who would now never become one of Nothing.

I became the widow of no one and presumed that my widowhood of nothing was what filled the silence in Father's mind. A foreigner of us, António was unaware of the lake's treachery.

Suddenly, I was reminded of Mother's prohibition from years before. Had I complied with it, perhaps I would not have lost the man who was to marry me, and my pain would only, and still, be the one of mourning Grandfather.

But had I obeyed, neither would I have become a woman nor learnt to feel me by feeling the other. Disobedience allowed me to find António and the love of the flesh. My head was spinning with endless shattered possibilities. The future was no longer a time for me.

António was buried in Vila Franca two days later.

All eyes felt sorrow for me. I detested people's commiseration. I felt shame on seeing António's coffin being put into the ground with him inside it: so young and so wasted. Our pain provided the people with a novel interlude in their daily lives, and I abhorred being at the core of a staged, pitiful, collective lamentation.

When I arrived at Nothing after the funeral, I gave orders for the lake to be enclosed. From now on it was not Mother forbidding me from going to the lake, it was I forbidding anyone to venture near the false waters. The fence would bar all access and, with time and forgetting, the footpath leading to the oak-gilded shores vanished into nothingness beneath a blanket of grass and bush. The lake died from our minds.

I stored my wedding gown in the chest of the brides of Nothing, I being the only bride of nothing. And I killed my marriage, burying it alongside António in the depths of my heart.

When I closed the chest, I felt I had a past.

Outside, vintage carried on.

VIII

Winter came dry. It was as though the still, false water which had taken António was being punished by free waters refusing to fall so as not to add to its falseness. To cheer me up a bit, Father had a couple of peacocks brought, and from then on there have been peacocks roaming the gardens of Nothing.

"The mournful sound of India," Mother said serenely about their strange mewing that echoed afar. I only realised from where she had taken that comparison when, years later, coming home from burying her, I opened the bookcase and found a copy of *A Passage to India* by E. M. Forster. That instant, left to myself in front of those special, secluded shelves, I could understand more clearly the world in which she lived: its remoteness and exoticisms, its pasts and its secrets. I was not surprised, in the discovery of her many books, that she was not one to live with us, preferring to seek exile from Nothing in a parallel world of her imagination. I think her soul still lives there.

Engrácia discovered it all when she realised my pads were not showing up to be washed. The news was bittersweet. To us it meant the perpetuation of Nothing. However, to the outside world, it meant my dishonour and the reason my wedding had been rushed. I had fallen, and the error was being amended. The ghosts of Margarida and Uncle Romano were resurrected from Father's memories, and he could guess that the foul tongues of the people would find in me a new source of gossip. My poor Father, who could not protect me.

The days went by after the confirmation of the news. Father did not chastise me, and Mother's silence was equal to her usual self. The recent past was not to be awakened. My son would be a son of Nothing and the barriers of Nothing were all that was needed to bring us further from António, the man because of whom I was stained, and from the people who insisted on my downfall.

Father had Nothing electrified. He wanted to welcome his grandson with light and every possible comfort that could render his orphanage less conspicuous. The electrification of the house kept us busy while I suffered the worst of day-long morning sickness — morning, afternoon and evening — throughout the eight months my son lived inside me.

In May, a premature birth falsely validated people's speculation that I had conceived before António had proposed. I presume such a thought must have surfaced in Father's mind. I neither confirmed nor denied. I did not feel like summoning the strength to engage in discussing a matter I had no interest for. I knew the truth. All else was irrelevant to me.

The pain came at night. Engrácia was the mother I did not have to cool my forehead with a wet towel and hold my hand while I pushed out that odd thing which had inhabited and deformed me.

The midwife, who had brought me into this world twenty years before, was called in from Ladeirinhas, but when she arrived one of the maids had already used the stove's flame to disinfect the large scissors Engrácia kept in her sewing box, and the cord had been cut.

I heard his crying of panic and cold, and thought about the pain of being born. For only a split second I was sorry the poor creature did not have a father and was going to grow up hearing about the body brought back from the lake before his mother could have been married. A shadow hovered over my heart, and I was scared for not knowing whether I would love that being or not. What if I was like Mother and could not find the space in my heart to love a child?

All my fears were dispelled when a bundle of person wrapped in soft, woolen lace blankets was put on my bosom. In his milky-white blue eyes I could read he was a son of Nothing. The bundle was mine. I held him with the strength drawn from a new form of love pouring out of my heart.

And then I wept all the tears I had not released when I lost António. I would not die without being called a mother.

"Let the tongues say a son has been born to Nothing!" Father exclaimed when, at daybreak, he came into my room to check on me and his grandson. I saw happiness stamped on his face. I, who had never seen his face glow with happy happiness before. I saw the three of us going for walks in the vineyards and him teaching his grandson to predict the weather and measure the seasons.

I fell asleep in the lightest, most satisfied sleep of my life.

Mother came to see us when the sun was already high in the sky.

"He is beautiful, my grandson," she stated, looking at the baby who was sleeping soundly, exhausted from having been born. "Call him António."

I assented and baptised my son with the name of the father. A few days later we took him to the baptismal font in the church at Ladeirinhas. Luísa had borne a child, but it was Matilde baptising him in all the solemnity of a paper. Would God recognise that it was my son and not hers?

I did not have milk for him. A wet nurse was accommodated in the room next to mine. She had had a baby girl some weeks before António was born, but I did not encourage a lot of contact with her for fear my son might grow attached to her as I had been to Engrácia.

By the time he turned eight months old I sent her away. Despite the circumstances of his birth which I thought could turn him into an embittered baby — my sad, nauseated pregnancy, his orphanhood, the weirdness of his grandmother — António was the most docile of little creatures. As though, out of respect for my unmarried mourning, he did not wish to upset me with crying and hunger out of hours.

At night, I bent over his crib or sat in the rocking chair holding him and just let myself be filled by his sweet smell.

Overwhelmed with joy, I realised that we come from an absolute nothing and that we are born lacking everything which makes us human and that everything has to be learnt. I loved my son in every little thing I saw him learn. I admired his every conquest.

And, most of all, I became fully aware of the new vocabulary invading my life. Mother would be uttered in relation to me, and I could use the word son preceded by the possessive my. My son.

A whole lexicon was added to the words I so loved to speak. Father would open his mouth to talk about his grandson inasmuch as I would say son because I was a mother. We would all be in the possession of new words, and that enriched us.

More than thinking I was a mother, I found it strange that Mother was a grandmother. There was nothing grandmotherly about her. She was cold, proud and distant. I used the word Mother as a name and not as a word relating to the function she had in my life. How was it that, all of a sudden, she was a grandmother? How could she be a grandmother without having been a mother? Grandmothers were meek and old, full of the life they have had. Mother had not aged yet. Her marble complexion was not growing wrinkly as Father's was by all the sun he was exposed to when he was in the fields. Mother was tall, and the way she always stood so upright would not allow her to come down to a child's level. It was very confounding for me to think of her as a grandmother and to have to teach my son to call her thus.

With Father, on the other hand, it was all very different. He was grandfather material, given his patience and infinite capacity for loving. His love was shared with us all, and he would give himself to my son just as if he had birthed him. Having Father by my side meant I would never be afraid of life ahead. António would be always protected by us and by Nothing.

There was nothing I feared. Eternity awaited me.

IX

Those were happy years. Just as happy were my son's infancy and my maternity. My maternity... Now when I say this and look back, I realise I was a mother. It all seems so distant now.

My son sweetened me, but at the very same time I became that sweetened person, I also became possessive of Nothing and of him. Having him increased my determination and courage. I believe I became a tad bossy and a lot more of a woman. Besides, just as Father was getting older, so too multiplied my responsibilities over Nothing.

Only with a clear mind and a strong will can one administer something like Nothing, and being a mother helped me take care of Nothing. Slowly, I was emerging from the chrysalis of Daughter of Manel from Nothing to stretch my wings as Luísa from Nothing.

Divided between my son and Nothing I had no time for my single heart. Those were not thoughts that crossed my mind nor did I have such urges. I felt fulfilled, and the labour of days provided me with the sound sleep of nights. I would fall asleep, lulled by the sweet joy of having a son in the room next door.

We taught him to ride and infused into him the love for Nothing. The model Father and Grandfather had used for me was now replicated in another generation.

My worst fear was that someday António might escape to the lake. Consequently I always had him under strict surveillance. The orders were clear for all: Under no, but absolutely no circumstance was anyone to lose sight of my son. Apart from that, António enjoyed all the ample space of Nothing to play, and he was a contented child.

Children will be children, so there were days when he would drive Engrácia crazy. Sometimes he would find a way to get into the chicken coops, looking for eggs, only to frighten the hens so badly they would stop laying. At others he would run after the peacocks to pluck their bright feathers.

At yet others, Engrácia would fret over him because he had been in the sun for too long, and that was not good for his young soft spot. Then she would sit him still and put a folded towel on his head to suck the sun out of his head with a glass full of water turned upside down on the towel. I was skeptical of those superstitions, but, the truth was, there rose bubbles of air while the glass of water was doing its job of draining out what Engrácia said was the accumulated sun in "the little child's head".

She also did not let the boy be exposed to moonlight in his sleep, as that would cause his eyeballs to turn around in their sockets. And she was afraid of other physical activities, such as jumping down from trees, because they were bad for his stomach.

I laughed at those worries and was only too keen to let Engrácia be in charge of the more burdensome tasks of raising my son. From him I received only the tenderness of someone who called me mother and smiled at me, eyes beaming with a child's loving passion. Those watery blue eyes, ours, specked with black from his father's side.

There were times when I sat him in front of me on the saddle, and we would venture into Nothing looking for jays and fox burrows. In summer we picked wild blackberries which grew in the thickets around old stone walls dividing the several properties that comprised Nothing. It gave me tremendous pleasure watching his small mouth and teeth be blackened by the berries he ate while his little fingers tried to pick them without being hurt by the thorns. Each time he picked a berry it was a moment of pride and jubilance that filled my heart with a new, vivific bliss of me towards him.

I loved him more than one can possibly love, and that may well have been my greatest arrogance. I let myself be dazzled by my love for him. Seldom was I reminded he had had a father, such was his happiness and mine.

Father was livelier now that he was a grandfather. He made his grandson wood rifles and told him he could hunt for crickets and grasshoppers with them. On the days Father went to Vila Franca to shop for the month's groceries, he took António with him and bought him licorice candies wrapped in cones of brown paper.

One day my son vanished. I took him for his nap, and when it was time to wake him he had disappeared from his bedroom.

I ran to the kitchen to sound the alarm, and we went looking for him in all the places he usually played. We searched the stables, the barn, the cellar. We went to the garden to see if he was there, chasing the peacocks. But nothing.

My heart was pounding out of my chest, and anxiety nearly stopped my breathing. I returned home to check whether he might be hiding under the bed or in some other room.

I found him, quietly sitting in Mother's room.

When I opened the door, I had the sense of intruding on a serene picture, like some old painting of a nostalgic moment. Mother had sat him on her lap, his back leaning against her and, very attentively, he was turning the pages of a book with colourful illustrations.

My relief was immense.

Then I was struck by a deep sadness, reminded that I had never sat on Mother's lap. I wanted to know why, but it was too late. The past was an ancient and closed space.

I shut the door and left without saying anything.

Somehow I found solace in that encounter of two such far-apart and disparate generations. And murmuring, I asked, I do not know of whom or what, that my son might not forget that moment.

The panic of the previous moments juxtaposed with the impossible portrait of grandmother and child shook my nerves and melted my beating heart. Behind that closed door, I cried, just as so many years before I had cried secretly so Father would not hear me.

It was around this time that Mother found out about my writings. She caught me one day when I was sitting at a small table under the shade of the leafy loquat tree in the backyard garden, facing the bedrooms. I was writing about happiness.

She had me called in. When I got to her study, she said she had no idea I wrote and asked whether I did that as a habit. I answered that it was nothing and, indeed, I had written my diaries since a bit before António was born. She moved from in front of the window, from where she had seen me and waited for me, and went to face the wall of the bookcase, whose doors she opened wide.

"The bottom shelf. You may use it."

She pointed downwards, letting me know that what I wrote was important and she wanted me to preserve my words, just as she preserved others' words.

I had fond thoughts for her in that moment, feelings which had always been absent from my heart when confronted by my own mother. Not that I considered her more of my mother for it: This was something different. My awkward, estranged mother was materialising as a person in front of me.

I was overcome by silence. Words failed me. I was unable to thank her for that surprising and profound gesture. I hastened to my bedroom to fetch the notebooks I had filled with António when I fell in love with him, and those I had been filling with the conquests of another, more of my own, António. My states of mind and soul had found their way into my diaries, the same way I wrote about the seasons that made Nothing alive and living in a perpetual cycle.

I snatched the diaries out of the drawer in my closet and thought about their new place of residence: A much loved and cared for bookcase in a little study filled with light, where they would be esteemed for the value of their words.

As I was often oblivious of those notebooks, I thought what was happening was a sort of promotion of their importance and had the thought that there were things in Nothing to which Mother paid attention, after all, as if, hovering over us without being seen, she possessed some kind of omniscient sight of everything.

After Nothing had been electrified, which was the first genuine modernization of the farm, there came a time for us to adjust to the times in other ways.

António was still a months-old baby when we started going to the seaside to Ericeira in August. It was a way for us to flee the stifling heat of the dry land of our valley. As soon as the cereal crops were harvested and just before vintage started, Father and I would take Mother and Engrácia to find refuge in a house we rented from year to year.

There, we could all enjoy the benefits of the iodine-laden sea air which was particularly healthy for the baby. In the first year, the wet nurse came with us. So, in the beginning of that arrangement we went to Ericeira by taxi. We settled in and, two days later, straight out from Nothing, there they arrived: the landau and the cart with provisions, our dishes and clothing, the stable and the errand boys, a maid and a cook.

We sojourned in the two-story house in whose backyard a lemon tree stood watch. By late afternoon, Father would take Mother and her silences to the village main square to have a *mazagran*[28] and listen to the sound of people.

And every year, his Monarchistic soul, nostalgic of a by-gone past, would repeat to exhaustion — ours, that is — the story of when His Majesty King *Dom* Manuel and Her Majesties Queen *Dona* Amélia and Queen *Dona* Maria Pia had to abandon the country, coming to Ericeira to embark on a ship into exile.[29] Poor King Manuel, who had escaped from the bombs and rifle shots of deposition by the skin of a tooth, as though he were a criminal, and the Republic, which was of no good to the country.

Later, when António was four years old, I began taking them to Ericeira by car. Father was going through another phase of modernising euphorias on account of his grandson.

He bought a radio set to be placed in the living room where we could listen to the Portuguese Radio Club,[30] which people on the farm, not knowing how to pronounce these strange new words, radio and club, called it "the Portuguese in the radio club".

In the evening we would usually sit together to listen to the

---

28. *Mazagran* is a refreshing drink made of coffee, lemon juice and, occasionally, a splash of rum, served with ice and lemon slices and sweetened to taste. It derives its name from a tall glass typical of the Argelian town of Mazagran where it was originally served.

29. After the Republican coup of 1910 which toppled the Monarchy, King *Dom* Manuel II, His Mother, Dowager Queen *Dona* Amélia and his paternal grandmother, Queen *Dona* Maria Pia, fled to Ericeira. There they boarded the royal yacht *Amélia* which took them to exile in England. The first years of the Portuguese Republican regime were characterised by much political instability and several failed attempts at restoring the Monarchy.

30. Founded in 1931, Rádio Clube Português was one of the first national radio stations in Portugal, and also the most popular.

wireless. Mother did not find sound particularly pleasing, so she rarely joined us. I, on the contrary, would sit António on my knees and enjoyed listening to the latest tunes and the news bulletins. It was in that communion with sound that, years later, we learned a new war was coming.

I remember one day in 1932 my Father furiously turning off the radio because he could not bear to listen to Salazar [31] making a speech on Radio Ajuda to celebrate the sixth birthday of the national revolution by which the country had passed from feeble Republic to fully-fledged dictatorship.

"Revolution. Which Revolution?!" he thundered. "Revolution would be to bring back to power the one who should rightfully be there!"

Suffice to say, we all left the room, because when he started to expound on his endearment for the Monarchy, we knew exactly what he was going to say.

The exiled King would die, a short few months afterwards, in July that same year.

The greatest novelty of that period was the car Father bought me: a Citroën 7CV Traction Avant, the ultimate thing in mechanical technology because of its front-wheel drive. People nicknamed it the Dragger and, on Sundays, when we went to Mass in Ladeirinhas, all the children ran in front of us yelling: "Here comes the Dragger! Here comes the Dragger!"

Father did not find such childish nonsense amusing, but I smiled broadly because António, in his tender age, thought all that noise must be a celebration and laughed like crazy. My heart was filled with sunny jubilation.

It did not take me long to learn to drive. Three gears were not that difficult to operate, and the car gave me a first glimpse of freedom in space and time and how that freedom translates into the freedom

---

31. António de Oliveira Salazar (1889-1970) was the founder and undisputed Prime-Minister of *Estado Novo* (New State) from 1932 to 1968. Under the authoritarian, right-wing government that ruled Portugal from 1932 to 1974, many civic liberties were denied, including freedom of assembly and the press. The Revolution of 24 April 1974 put an end to the *Estado Novo* regime.

of us.

Freedom became my addiction. I would go to Vila Franca and back in an instant when I had some errand to run. And, whenever I felt like it, I would go out alone or take António with me to show him the Tagus or climb the Montejunto. On holidays in Ericeira, it became a habit for me to take us all out to Sintra to eat *queijadas*[32] or to see the wild sea from the promontory at Cape Roca, the westernmost tip of mainland Europe.

I enjoyed driving and, with hindsight, I believe when I went out with the car just because I was in the mood for it, I must have experienced the same plethora of sensations Mother did when, out of the blue, she went for her walks about which we knew nothing. I was her daughter, after all.

---

32. Typical, regional tartlets.

X

I blame it on your envy and on my excessive wanting. One should never want too much. I should already know that. Stubborn, I never learned. Each and every time, I never learned.

It was mid-July, and I could hardly wait for August's interlude in Ericeira. I was living in the sweet anticipation of the coming happier days, happier still than those in the sequence of happy days and laborious routines that made my life in Nothing.

We had sown a black-bearded variety of hard wheat which we would then sell to the Industrial Company of Portugal and Colonies, or Nacional,[33] for the production of dried pasta. Only after Mother's death would I discover some biographical notes relating to Fernando Pessoa, our genius bard of the twentieth century, and realise he worked for Nacional as a correspondent in foreign languages. Struck by the coincidence, I would thereafter imagine the prosaic of our farm and our wheat marginally entangled in the life of a poet who was anything but prosaic.

That summer the agricultural year was being good for both irrigated and cereal crops, and I was busy with the account books which had become more complex and demanding after we acquired the properties of Antão and Corço and thereby added to Nothing's work and manpower. Father, already lacking the patience for record keeping and papers, was only too keen to hand over to me the dullness of bureaucracy, preferring instead to be in the fields, managing the things he had always enjoyed.

Between the kitchen and the living-room there was an old butler's pantry where we kept, under lock and key, the reams of papers pertaining to Nothing. I was there, concentrating on numbers and doing the math on how much we would profit from selling the wheat

---

33. Nacional is a Portuguese company dating back to 1849, specialising in the processing of cereals for human consumption that range from flours to pastas, noodles and assorted biscuits. From 1919 to the 1980s it was also called Companhia Industrial de Portugal e Colónias (CIPC).

when Engrácia came rushing in, screaming and pulling her hair.

"O, my poor Child! O, my poor Child!"

I tried to calm her down, to make her say something more than "O, my poor Child!" but she pulled me by the hand, forced me outside the house and made me run toward the wheat field. My heart was thinking Father and what might have happened to him. I got to the stubble field and kept running without minding where I put my feet, hasting to the pile of wheat sheaves waiting to be threshed. There a multitude of reapers was already gathered.

"O, my poor Child, he wanted to climb up the pile. O, my poor Child!" Engrácia's excruciating cries clouded my mind.

What I saw was You. You were there in front of me, in your serene wholeness. Standing behind him, yours was the clearest presence among the cries, my pain and their anguished faces. I wished you to take me. That would have been the sweet hemlock of my will. I wanted anything but to see you in such contented exultation.

My son lay on the ground with nothing beneath him but the prickly stubble piercing against his soft skin. His hair was entangled in rough awns, but he was not asleep. My son was not sleeping.

I lifted the slack body of his five years of age, just finished dying, into my arms. I embraced him with the strongest strength I had. I wanted him to hear me. I wanted to tell him everything my wrenching womb was saying, and I wanted him to come back. My God, let my son be Lazarus.

I wished I were dreaming.

Looking up, I saw the white flag with which he had climbed to the top of the pile of sheaves. It was dancing in the wind. He had planted it there, as would some explorer on the summit of a mountain. And he had fallen, suffocating in the midst of the mass of wheatears and stalks of straw.

He was still warm. I smelled his sweet, familiar smell, and a dark hole opened beneath me. I did not want him to grow cold and leave me.

I screamed, and my screams dimmed Engrácia's. I died. I died in that so desolate pain. I died that day and never resurrected.

You cannot take me because I am dead, and that is why you linger there at the corner in that vain contemplation.

My crying was inconsolable. Bent with my knees on the ground, holding the corpse of the child I had delivered, I felt my heart was being torn in shreds. Such pain, however, was nothing compared to knowing that my son had died, and I had to go on living without him. It was all too definitive. All too final. All too finished and sealed. Nothing could possibly have that degree of end. It could not be like that.

It was impossible that I could get used to his not playing anymore, or not taking a nap, or not running to me. It was impossible that I would no longer ride with him on my saddle looking for jays, or that we would no longer take him to Ericeira and expose him to the wonders of the air of that wild sea.

My son could not be dead. And his hands holding mine: Was I never to feel his sweaty, warm little hands in mine? Or see the world opening wide before his eyes. Was I not to see that ever again?

When Father arrived, I thought I would have to oversee two burials. His legs gave way, and he fell helpless onto the rough stubble. The men came to his aid, and I could hear him crying, "O, God, it's terrible. O, God, it's terrible." Like me, he was crying inconsolably.

My son was Nothing and Nothing was my son. I had nothing left of nothing and I wanted nothing, not now, not ever. All these years later and I still find it difficult to believe I lost my son. The same way I can hardly believe I had him. Those five years were my whole life.

I got up from the stubbled ground and found the way home to the house, asking first for the bells to start tolling and then that water be heated so I could bathe my son.

I locked myself in the bedroom with him as I usually did at the end of the day. I washed him in the gently warmed water, dressed him and combed his fine hair. Then I sat with him on my lap and rocked him to sleep in the soothing relaxation after a long day playing.

They took him from my arms only when the coffin arrived and

was placed in the centre of the living-room so his mourning could begin. He looked like an angel: beautiful. The son that I kissed dead and cold, and from whom I could not, and did not want to part.

Father showed no signs of life. Sitting on a chair next to mine, he had aged a hundred years, the infinite, in the space of a few hours. Nothing had also ended for him.

Mother stared at an indistinct void in a far horizon which was not visible to us. She said nothing and wept not. I imagine my pain ached her, just as she hurt for Father's pain and the pain of Nothing. And I imagine that, ultimately, she ached with her own pain. Only there was nothing coming out from inside of her. Pain was kept within that, silent, closed container which was impenetrable to us.

As the hours passed, tears began to dry and my face started to crumple from the pain-laden, turbulent rivers of salt I had shed.

I endured the wake, the funeral mass, the priest, the procession to the cemetery, the old mourners, and even Engrácia comforting me in the desperate love of dismay. I endured it all and only regained consciousness that everything ended then and there, that my son had really died, when they opened the vault of the Boshoff where we were to lay the white casket with its gold-trimmed edges in which my son would rest for the utmost forever; endless and irretrievable.

I burst into convulsive tears at the prospect that when the door of the vault was shut, it was my son who was going to be left there while I had to face a journey back to Nothing, and I was alive.

I had gone to Ladeirinhas to bury a son. Nothing in this world compares to the pain of a parent burying her blood before its time.

Once again Matilde came to haunt me.

I was the one burying a child but in the eyes of the Law, the son was hers. In the blank they had to fill with the name of the mother on my son's death certificate, it was not my name that was there. It was the name of a somebody I did not recognise but who, all throughout my existence, had played the leading role of the life I lived. Ceremony belonged to Matilde; life was Luísa's.

In the harsh, long days that followed, I had the door to my son's bedroom cemented, creating a vacuum, a non-space, in Nothing.

I left everything as it had been during my son's brief life. It was far too painful to see his toys or smell the sheets of his bed when I looked for traces of his presence. That only made his absence more real, and I could not handle it.

The cemented door disappeared under a coat of paint. No one today notices that between my bedroom and that which belonged to Mother there is an air chamber where, once, my son lived. Sometimes I catch myself wondering how that room, suspended in a time of dust and old memories, might look now, and I try to visualise how it was when my son inhabited it. It is all in vain, and I live better ignoring my heart when it wants to recall such things.

They must have thought I was going crazy, but nobody dared oppose the door of António's room being sealed for all eternity.

In the quiet, somber faces I read the strangeness of my determination entwined with the understanding of the immeasurable pain which led me to do those things. They must have also feared that I had turned into Mother. After all, these were all symptoms of a colossal derangement, and my nerves could well collapse under such pressure.

In addition to having all traces of the room obliterated, I also had António's father exhumed and transferred into our vault in Ladeirinhas.

His father, the judge, probably thought I was losing my wits, but he acquiesced to my request. After all, he had also lost a grandson who he had never for a minute doubted to be his. And much like me too, he knew what it was to mourn a son. I could not bear to think of my son alone in the vault. The idea of his facing the loneliness of death was too much for me to cope with. Therefore I decided that his father would keep him company and protect him against the cold of the tomb.

It was a dismal procession, the one bringing the hearse with António's remains to Ladeirinhas. My orders were that the father's coffin was to be placed two shelves below the son's so the shelf in the middle could be left waiting for me. Father and son would thus meet in death.

After turning the key to lock the cast iron and glass door of the vault, I turned back to face a life of nothing, with no other prospect than to walk a long walk in the dark valley of shadows. I, dead, would walk.

One day they would lay me between the father and the son.

XI

I have no other recollections of that summer. I ignored whether we sold the wheat to good profit or not, or how was vintage, and if the wine was good. I know it was the last year we sowed wheat. From then on we began growing only forage crops, such as vetch or fenugreek, and invested in lesser cereals like barley, as if wheat had been the culprit in my son's death. Never again was Nothing to produce wheat; never for as long as it took me to purge the memory of my son. So, in the eternity that my life could be, wheat was an impossibility in Nothing. We also did not go to Ericeira, because all reasons to had died.

I kept myself busy with my mourning of madness, deciding what to do with my corpses and doing away with what connected me to them. When the door had been walled up with bricks and António, the father, had been transferred, I wanted to hold someone accountable for so irrecoverable a loss. So much and so often had I insisted that no one was to lose sight of my son. Ironic that I had forbidden him from getting near the lake and still he had drowned to his death. I blamed myself for not having always kept a close watch over him and still less on that day.

More gruesome, however, was the thought lurking in my head: Was it possible that, in forbidding me from going to the lake so many years before, Mother had anticipated the death of António, the father, and consequently that of António, the son of Nothing? I think Mother had foreseen the tragedy which had befallen us at that moment. Mother had tried to protect me by warding off my destiny, and now I was paying for my disobedience with life: mine and that of my son.

That summer I learnt that to love is to hurt and that hurting is always the reflection of the omnipresent presence of loss. I did not want to love again so I would never hurt. I wanted my heart to be hermetically shut. I wanted to distance myself from everything, as Mother had. How I envied her in her horizons beyond the horizon.

I determined to feel no more.

I longed for the wildness of the sea, storms of wind and rain to be mixed with my tears. I longed for untamed things that reminded me that I was alive when I was dead. It was not feelings I craved. My desire was rather for strong sensations the likes of going about naked amidst storms. I wanted to feel my body beaten by heavy and cold rain. I wanted things that ripped my oppressed chest.

October came. I picked myself up, rented the house in Ericeira where, every summer of my son's life, we had sojourned and where we had not been this last summer spent in death, and drove off.

I left alone, and everyone in Nothing must have thought I was becoming like Mother. They let me go, though. No questions were asked; no obstacles raised, for nobody dared interfere with my pain.

In the low season, the humble village resembled a desert of souls. Everything was closed, which, for me, was actually quite comforting. I needed the loneliness, the open spaces, the lack of words from people's mouths. I wanted the wild sea of angry waves of foam and the deep blue of death. I wanted my silence for company. I wanted to run away from everything and from Nothing.

Several days I spent without seeing anyone. I hired a local girl to clean the house and take care of the cooking but requested her services for only every other day as I did not have the patience for having a maid around. Sometimes I would go barefoot across the desolate expanses of cold, wet sand. Or, going to the Northern Beach, I would walk along the tidal line where the surf of that wild sea came breaking. At others, I would lean against the thick wall of the village and just stand there staring at the distant infinite where the sea touches the sky.

Never had I been nor was I ever again so alone and lonely. I felt my body was nothing more than a hollow, soulless shell. My mind was not residing in me but in the far away distance where everything ends and everything begins and which was now the point beyond the horizon where my gaze rested. Life was a kind of trance, and oftentimes I would find myself at a place and have no idea how I had gone there. Living was a mechanical activity bearing no connection to my self.

Rarely did I have the lucidity of now. I was a new species to Nothing, in a limbo between Argentina's absentmindness and Mother's alienation. Perhaps we were all afflicted by some form of derangement, passed on genetically. And, in the end, I was nothing more and nothing less than the latest link in the chain of daughters of Nothing to bear that burden. In my particular instance, the demential eruption had a tangible cause: the death of my son, the orphan of my non-husband. It was as though the fibers of my sanity had slackened and I embraced the insanity which characterised us: old Argentina and my so unfathomable Mother. And now me.

"Don't think about it anymore."

The voice woke me from my pensive slumber. I was at the wall in yet another contemplative moment of infinite nothing. I looked sideways to where the voice was coming from, and I saw a man in his thirties, wearing tinted glass spectacles and holding an umbrella.

Unware that I had been standing in the rain, I was suddenly conscious of the drizzle of rain and sea water, falling over me from the skies. My hair was dripping down my cheeks. I thought he was somewhat odd and lonely in the surrounding loneliness of the empty village. An exotic man wearing dark glasses on a day of greyish sea and greyish sky.

"Come on, don't think about it; take shelter here," spoke again the man, who seemed as blue as the day and as my soul.

Words had not come out of me in a long time, and so I was not able to find the voice with which to make them at that moment. I assented and allowed him to lend me the protection of his wide, black umbrella with its varnished bamboo handle. He offered to escort me home, and my instinctive steps guided us in the silence of the way.

When he told me goodbye at the gate, he declared he would stop over the following day to make sure I had not fallen ill from the autumn rain.

I climbed the step between the gate and the street and lingered there, watching the stranger disappear into the distance which had brought him hither. I thought I had been in the presence of an apparition and that my world was no longer this.

I only discovered I had not imagined the scene the following day when the bell rang and, from the window, I saw the stranger with the dark glasses being true to the promise he had made the day before.

I descended the stairs to say hello and to thank him for having brought me home. I knew the words would come out of me.

He introduced himself as Antero de Novaes. He was a lawyer in Lisbon and was staying in Ericeira to get relief for his wife's asthma and her constant fatigue brought about by her illness. He was very glad to see me well, and it was wonderful how the weather today was so different from yesterday.

I told him nothing about myself except that I was Luísa and I was on holidays. The courtesy did not last longer than five minutes, and we bid farewell with the polite intention of an, "I'll see you around, then".

It so happens that, sometimes, the coincidence of intentions is engraved in one's destiny. Two days after our interlude at the gate, I saw him walk with his wife in the village's central park where I was sitting, engaged in the pseudo-catharsis of writing the essence of infinite loss in my diary.

He greeted me amiably and introduced me to his wife, a dwarfish and pale little woman, all covered in lace and cardigans so as to catch neither cold, nor the sun, nor light, nor rain.

I greeted her with a handshake and felt the lace of her glove and her light and wilted hand. She was a weary woman, one of those who accommodates the chronic condition of being ill and embraces that as a way of life. Job: patient. They walked away, and I forgot them.

Once in a while I got news from Nothing. Short letters from Father, written with the insecure and coarse handwriting of someone who had not studied beyond the second grade because childhood had been spent in duties other than school. He wrote about the farm, the first rains, the ditches and furrows which had to be dug in autumn to drain the waters, the pruning season beginning, the tasting of the new wine and the quantity of brandy to be distilled. The small details of our rural livelihood. Unaccustomed to letters, they bewildered him for their excessive formality and, fearing their noble character and official tone, he only wrote about prosaic, petty things. He hoped I was well and that I could return home before long.

My heart lit up with the warmth of Nothing that came to me via the crooked handwriting of Father's unsharpened pencil.

I received only one letter from Mother, which, given its unexpectedness, caught me by surprise. Unlike Father's letters, I could not make myself open it the instant the postman passed by late in the morning.

What would that woman have to tell me? What had her soul found so necessary to write to me? Obviously she would not give me the news of Nothing or tell me about the affairs that kept the farm busy for she had no idea what the hard work of Nothing was.

The remainder of the day was spent in the curiosity of the words written on that letter but without the impulse of will that made me open it.

As was becoming usual in my Ericeira sojourn, by late afternoon I went to the wall facing the ocean to watch the sunset and took the letter with me. I opened it with the wind smelling of seaweed and waves hitting my face.

Nothing, 2 November 1936

My Daughter,

I hope this letter can find you in better spirits. I do not wish to upset your retreat or worry your heart, we are fine here, the living and the deceased. Yesterday, by All Saints', Daddy and I had Mass celebrated for your beloved departed. You have them, dear Daughter, overabundantly for your tender years. More will come, as we all who cross this life of deceit know. However, days will also come when the joys of the living will lessen the pain of so irreparable losses. All that begins has an ending, my Daughter. Such is our nature and the nature of things.

Come back when your heart tells you it is time to come back, if ever your heart tells you that.

From your Mother, in great esteem,

Máxima

I collapsed. I cried over the Mother I did not know. I cried for me and for the deceased that were rightfully mine as she so lucidly made clear to me. I cried because, in the silence of her words written in permanent ink and educated handwriting, so distinct from Father's, my Mother spoke to the deepest within me. In a woman of mute words, her speech was silent and yet it said a thousand more things than the words I uttered in the sound of my voice.

Mother was not rushing my return to Nothing. She was not even suggesting I was bound to return. Her gift was an open-ended choice subject to my own free will and my will alone. That was simply the greatest freedom that had ever been bestowed upon me. My seclusion-loving Mother was offering me the supreme freedom of not going back to Nothing if such was my wish. In that one letter she let me know she would understand and support whatever decision I made, even if my decision was actually not going back. Unlike Father, Mother had written, not to tell me about Nothing, but to talk to me. In her letter it was I as a person who was important for her: I as Matilde, the name she had forced on me.

I folded the letter and pressed it against my chest while watching the last rays of sun sink beyond the distant sea. For the first time in my life I felt I was the daughter of two parents. Far away, in my ancestral Nothing, there were two beings whose daughter I was and, for the first time since my son's death, I did not feel overpowered by the desolate loneliness in which my soul, my heart and my sore inner self lived. I was the orphan of a son but daughter of living father and mother.

I ran across him one morning by the water's edge at the beach in Praia Sul. He was walking alone in the refuge of his thoughts. His dark glasses and the big black umbrella he used as a cane gave him a soberly elegant look. A lone, thin figure of a man in the landscape. The whitish, damp mist rendered the clarity of the day diffuse and muffled the rumble of waves in the low tide.

We greeted in and about the coincidence. Lonelinesses and sadnesses of soul connected us. Grief was a language we both spoke. Therefore, elaborate conversation was useless and redundant for us to understand why we were both there at that hour or why we were spending some time in the cloudy cold of an empty village. He knew nothing of my motives and I knew little of his. I knew about his wife's expectorating asthma but was ignorant of what his heart harboured. There was no need to know reasons. We recognised one another as peers and, maybe because of that, we did not find it necessary to fill the moment with words. Little by little, life was making sure to teach me that the language of silence communicated as much or even more than the language spoken through the sound of words.

He kissed me out of longing and volition. I reciprocated, overwhelmed by an urgency whirling inside of me like a stormy sea. I felt his tongue wanting me and I gave him of me as his whole was asking. Unabashed by shame, his hands ran swiftly through my waist and the contours of my breasts and I awoke the dormant woman who had succumbed to the pain of successive losses. It was my body that felt. The hollow cocoon was being filled with me and I kissed him avidly, hearing nothing other than our panting breaths entangled in one another and the faint, rolling sound of soft waves breaking on the wet sand.

We parted our mouths and stood still in the embrace of those who want the other for the first time. Shame or the awkward embarrassment of a kiss between strangers did not cross our minds. He told me he wanted to be with me but that, first, he had to tend to his wife, so I told him I would be at home waiting for him after his obligations were finished.

I let loose of the embrace and ran across the beach and the steep little road leading to the village. I ran nonstop and out of breath. I ran out of freedom and promise. I ran full of energy.

Ugly words of adultery and sin were not in my mind when he

walked through the gate. The afternoon had revealed a pale sun which had timidly vanquished the morning mist. All of me wanted that. Never have I carried any regrets about a moment that was kept in my memory as the time when my body was given as the utmost offer. In return, I received the most the other had to give. Nothing was wrong. Nothing was evil. There was no sin and there were no bindings of morals. Freedom was that.

I opened the door of the corridor to let him in and he took me right there and then. He unbuttoned my shirt, bit my lips out of hunger and lifted my skirt with determined, hasty hands. Incapable of the lucidity of touch, my hands got lost in his body. Feeling was too much to feel. In my dead soul, the body was mine for that instant, the sensation was mine. I closed my eyes so I could be shut to the outside of me and could only feel. Then we fell on the floor. Exhausted, weak, dishevelled bodies. I could only be happy in my body, and I was. The soul which had abandoned me months before was not there in that corridor. Nevertheless, my cocoon had been filled and the pain of emptiness had been appeased for a moment.

The following days he always showed up at the same time, and always at the same time we took one another. In the bedroom, he would undress me in the slow motion of someone who is no longer in a rush.

I had never been naked in front of a man before, but I found a sensual contentment in feeling my body scoured by a new gaze, a gaze of wanting. I discovered skin in its plenitude of beautiful. I did not love him, although I loved his body in each and every piece I explored. I was happy in the velvety hedonism of long afternoons in an unmade bed and of skins glowing with the perspiration of sensuousness.

Yes, it was impossible for me to love him. Looking back I am grateful that he showed me how good it is to feel. I had promised myself never to love again in order not to suffer and, consequently, what I felt in those afternoons had nothing to do with love. Moreover, I was far too hurt to be able to feel with my soul and my heart. The only thing I had left was my body. Only that piece of me could feel anything. It was not the rain falling on me without my noticing it.

I was numb to those outer sensations. What my body could feel back then was something different, something that could only be that undressing and that pleasurable giving and taking. To feel in that particular way was all I was capable of, and all that was enough and more than enough for me.

I said goodbye to him at Cabo da Roca,[34] the westernmost promontory in the whole of continental Europe. Without telling him the whys, I arranged for us to meet at a place where the sea was at its wildest on an afternoon after the many afternoons we had spent, taken away by the sound of distant waves and shared respirations which were the lullaby of our togetherness.

In front of the immensity of the wide ocean, he looked like a surreal figure coming from a time which was not my own. Upright and motionless, his pitch-black hair was dancing in the breeze and his dark glasses, which protected his clear-water eyes, added to the exoticism of his frame. Indeed, his eyes were so like mine; too sensitive and hurt by the glare.

"You're leaving," he ascertained. I nodded in assent and kissed him with the strength of things final. I bid farewell to the body which would touch me no more and no longer get to the deepest of my uninhabited cocoon. In that kiss I bestowed all my gratitude and the future memory I would take back with me to the forever that now stood before me.

Nothing awaited me.

---

34. Cabo da Roca is the westernmost place on mainland Europe. Translated, "Cabo" means Cape; "Roca" is a big rock or rocky promontory.

XII

I embraced Father and noticed old age creeping in through the suffering of his soul, emaciating his body. I smelled the aroma of the open air of Nothing coming from his clothes and from his skin, the sun and earth.

I was home.

My mind preserved that embrace of love, an embrace so different from the embraces in which I had lived lately, embraces of body and the senses so distinct from the warm and serene embrace of my Father of all times. Engrácia wiped her tears with the tip of her apron while stammering that her Child had returned.

My whole world was Nothing.

I went up to Mother's study to greet her in the distanced cordiality which characterised our relationship. The letter had been an episode made possible by the remoteness of presence and the letters on paper, allowing us to say more than the words spoken face to face. In the physicality of proximity, nothing had changed, and she and I remained the familiar strangers we always were.

"Welcome, my Daughter," she said, not asking for news of me or showing an interest in the cure, or not, of my emotional ailments. She looked at me with her usual vague eyes which did not let me know whether she saw in me her returned daughter, the sore woman or some other person who had meantime been born.

I failed to comprehend whether she was examining me in search of little things, such as my being thinner or more tanned from the salty sun or older in my complexion. I know not. I never managed to realise what it was that she saw.

"Thank you, Mother," I replied and finished off my courtesy visit.

I was back, I thought, while inhaling deeply the air of the house after closing the door to Mother's room behind me. I felt I was among mine. Even Mother's strangeness, known to me from birth and for its constancy, was a natural thing.

However, Nothing was void to me. Without my son, Nothing was nothing more than a lifeless farm, a piece of land of abundant work and endless responsibilities and nothing else. The immateriality that shaped Nothing into form had crumbled, and now I could only see its tangibility, co-substantiated in tillage, harvests, seeds, wine and olive oil.

The rains set in: the mist and the short days of humidity and cold. Nothing was bracing for the wintry season of bare trees and dormant vines. The desolate scenery was soothing to my bleak soul.

I did not do much that winter. My mind kept revisiting the touch my body had felt. There was little to write about in a semi-hibernating farm. Still, I wrote the little there was to write about our daily lives and preferred to keep in my mind the pictures of my shared body in a faraway place by the sea than to commit them to writing.

In the days the clouds gave us some truce from the rain, I rode on horseback, and away into the vineyards I went, where groups of men were pruning the vines and women were busy picking the twigs which were then burnt in piles of grey, rough smoke. I talked to them colloquially about the trivialities of farm work and the fields. In return I was greeted with the mirth of people who derived no evil and no boredom in brawny work and, instead, fill the chilly morning air with laughter and singing, people who derive joy in the simplest things, such as a slice of bread or a glass of wine.

The humbleness of country folk always struck me as grand, and I always treated it with respect. From within my privileges, even those of my feeling pain, I always looked at those people who worked for us and toiled our fields with profound deference and humility. They buried their dead, just as I buried mine; they mourned just as I did, and yet they had the amazing capacity to sing while beating olive trees with a pole on frosty mornings and their fingers hurt from the cold, or while they were pruning the vines or hoeing.

As the daughter of Nothing, I could take refuge in deserted beaches to cultivate my grief. Privileged as I was, I was allowed not to bury my pain as those people were forced to. To watch the men and women who gave life to Nothing was healthy to my anguished soul. On seeing those bent-over women picking the twigs left from pruning, I could not help but wonder how many of them had not already buried their children. Some could even have buried more than one. What would they feel? What part of their sorrow would not be akin to mine?

I refrained from asking and watched from a distance, not letting the thoughts be put into words. Nevertheless, I ached constantly; I was now a childless mother. Even if I was privileged in relation to those women, pain was a right I also had. Pain, albeit amidst material comforts, does not hurt less. There are no smaller and no bigger pains. There is pain. My memory-full, sleepless nights, my powerlessness to change the past, were the private ground of a pain which was exclusively mine and hence not subject to comparison with the pain of other human beings. Each of us carries private, individual suffering. I carried mine.

Winter was giving way to spring when the Marquis of Cabreza paid us a visit. He wanted to buy our wine production. Father took him to see the vineyards that were sprouting in the full bloom of light-green, tender leaves. The weather permitting, it would be a favourable year, and our wine always had good volume. It was not usual for us to sell the wine in bulk, but if the Marquis proposed a fair deal, surely we could do business.

The farms of the Marquis were located in the vicinity of Azambuja. He raised wild cattle [35] and produced a light wine quite distinct from our darker, more full-bodied variety. He was overflowing with plans to start a more serious wine business, having been inspired by a trip to France where he had had the opportunity of learning more about the trade. Taken up with a keen liking for doing business with us, his visits became more frequent.

Sometimes Father invited him to join us for supper. The Marquis loved bullfights and hunting, enjoyed a bit of a drink and played a good knife and fork. He petted my Father on the shoulders, but

---

35. "Wild cattle" is the term given to the specific kind of cattle bred for bullfighting in countries where that tradition exists.

somehow I did not appreciate his audible fondness for life, perhaps because my pain longed for the selfishness of discomfort. Or maybe it was because my dead soul could not stand to be close to living souls, and his gushed with life. His wife had died of a tumour the year before. He had three children bordering their teens and lived in a house of plenty. Like my Father, he was a committed champion of the royal cause; neither could it be otherwise for a marquis.

"Don't you think it would be a good idea?"

The subject popped up at dusk when Father and I were taking the horses and making our rounds of the farm to check the progress of late afternoon chores. Gently and carefully, he was letting me know that His Lordship, the Marquis, had feelings for me and was wanting to engage in a serious relationship with me. Father was playing the scout, charged with sounding out my opinion.

"Hence the frequent visits!," I bluntly retorted.

I was not in the least pleased to know of the Marquis's interest, despite my suspicion of it. And it infuriated me that he had neared my Father in order to get to me. That was sheer impudence. Father could tell the gentleman I was not up for it. He could even be nice and tell him I appreciated his interest but that, "No, Sir," I had no such feelings for him. Father did not insist and we resumed our way, a bit struck by the discomfort such a conversation caused.

During supper the following evening, Father picked up the subject again.

"But Daughter, it would be nice for you," he started.

"Daddy, I've already said no and, no, I don't want to hear about it anymore. Let's just forget it."

"A house like that, darling. There's nothing you could wish for that you wouldn't have. I'd be so relieved and you would be a marchioness. Imagine that."

"So that's it, me being a marchioness!" I exclaimed, out of discontent and blood about to boil in my veins.

"Of course, that's not it. But age is unforgiving, Daughter, and I won't last forever. Who's going to look after you when I'm gone? And who's going to help you with Nothing?"

I noticed he made no allusion to my Mother's presence in my

life. Were she to survive Father, she would not help me in the management of Nothing. She would not raise a hand to take care of me if he closed his eyes and she remained here.

"I don't need anyone to look after me and who told you you're going to die?"

"But darling, it's life. There was a time you thought about marrying. Wouldn't you like to do it now?"

"No, Father. I don't need to marry."

"This gentleman likes you. And he can give you a life you won't have here."

"Indeed, and I'm going to end up raising his children," I rebutted in anger. My son had died and never, ever, would I raise someone else's children. Never. Such was my selfishness, and I was entitled to it. It would hurt me beyond measure to live with somebody who had children, and my heart would simply not endure being put to that overwhelming test. I would not raise children not born out of me. It would be a betrayal to my son if ever such a thing came to happen. I would betray my son raising children who were nothing to me.

"Then they would be the ones to inherit Nothing. No way!" I continued.

"Don't say that. Your children would inherit Nothing."

Father tried to appease me, knowing, however, that female succession was not entirely protected under the law in a society defined back then by a patriarchy for which women only existed as someone's daughters or someone's wives.

"Only those born unto Nothing, inherit Nothing, my Father. Mark my words when I say that never in my life will I be a marchioness and be subjected to a man, let alone a man with children. To marry that gentleman is to lose Nothing and to lose Nothing is to kill me. For the last time, Father, I don't want to hear about this ever again."

I laid down my knife and fork, appetite having abandoned me, and took a sip of the wine of Nothing, to calm me and enjoy the liquid that made me who I was and which made us Nothing.

Silence set in, and I thought about the letter Mother had sent me in Ericeira during the worst stage of my mourning. The Mother who had written to tell me I was free to come back to Nothing only if my heart desired would surely understand me now. The Mother who had let me know my freedom was above all and any wish outside of me would support me now when I was fighting against the intents of a marquis in order to pursue my destiny as a single, unmarried woman. No, I had no need for a man, because that would abase me. Besides, after all I had lost, which was an absolute everything, I only had the shell I called body and Nothing. The little or nothing I had left, I was not going to lose.

XIII

In the summer, I received a package in the mail. Placed on the desk of the pantry we used as an office for the immense paperwork of Nothing, it was waiting for me one late afternoon after the watering of the plants had been done.

It was addressed to Luísa from Nothing, Nothing Estate, Vila Franca.

Whoever was writing to me was certainly unaware of my real name and did not have the slightest idea that our proper address was simply Nothing, Ladeirinhas, and then Vila Franca.

Not without curiosity, I opened the small cardboard package.

I was struck dumb and abruptly sat down—the reflex caused by my surprise.

Inside, a pair of dark brown, tinted glasses and a note folded in two.

So you see the world through other colours and shades,

Antero

Antero...

I remembered things. Thoughts were awakened. Immediately I was transported to a horizon of ocean and sea air. Antero had remembered me and was sending me a pair of glasses so the glare would not hurt my eyes again. I have worn them ever since.

Pleasant, constraint-free memories live in these glasses. Whatever happy memories I keep of my past life are not associated with sorrow and loss.

And, at that time, I feared happiness, for it had always ended in loss. To me, happiness was pain. The happiness of my son, my dead son. The walks with Grandfather which were no longer. The discovery of love, abbreviated by tragedy. All my happinesses were shrouded in an aura of pain.

All but the ones associated with Antero.

When I think of it now, it is still true that I remember Antero without suffering. Nothing did I ask of him, nothing did I expect and therefore I was happy in whatever the loss of me through the loss of my son — my death — may have brought joy for our having met.

Antero, who knew more of me than anyone else knew; Antero, who had been closer to me in the most private recess of my intimacy: Antero had established some sort of communication to let me realise I existed in a particular and untouched niche of his life, which had meantime carried on.

Our afternoons were locked in a past free of questions, attachments, or recriminations. I was there in this past of his as he was in mine. Sending me the glasses was proof that he thought of me on occasion as I sporadically thought of him. Those glasses attested to our having existed and that we had played an unforgettable role in each other's lives.

There was no return address on the envelope. No contact was to be expected from then onwards.

I held the little box to my chest and, almost imperceptibly, through the air of Nothing, sent him a whisper of gratitude.

"Thank you..."

My days and years went on. The Marquis of Cabreza never closed the wine deal with us. A pressure, however, was thickening over me; a dense cloud of unsaid words and fears. I could sense Engrácia's eyes on me. The veiled worries surfaced on Father's face. It was as though they were waiting for me to make a decision. And the decision was my getting married in order to produce the heir of Nothing. They felt the line dying out and looked to me as the one and only possibility of Nothing not ending as nothing.

I was the Grail of the land, the vessel for the blood, and I was not making up my mind. My obligation was to deliver an heir to Nothing, one who lived and bred after me. That was oppressive. It could not be my shoulders to carry that burden and I regretted not having someone who was willing to remove that cup of responsibility from me.

Time was running out fast, and I was supposed to catch up with it. I even blamed Mother for my state of oppression. Had she fulfilled her mission a little bit better, I would have siblings to relieve me from the burden of the succession of Nothing. But no, Mother was untouchable, and now it was up for me to solve the situation she had created. I was supposed to secure the future.

Time was a hangman. It imprisoned me in decisions I did not wish to make and, all around us, it was taking over the world in a new era of darkness.

Spain was being torn apart by internal fighting. Far away, and yet so frighteningly near, evil regimes were rising from the rubble. All breath was suspended in the anticipation of war. Every day we heard on the radio the dreadful news of an immense abroad where peace was being lost. We felt safe in the haven of Nothing, but we could sense storms forming beyond the horizon.

Without our realising, we started to listen to the news, ourselves immersed in an eerie silence of unbeating hearts. Our gaze was low, and it was almost as if our only sense was that of hearing.

In those moments spent around the radio set, our thoughts were halted, our souls hovered motionless, and we waited for something. We knew what it was without knowing exactly what it really was. Those were strange times.

XIV

The April rains of 1940 brought blood. I did not hear the rainfall. It fell velvety and silent while I was busy in the pantry-office, where more and more of my time was spent. No sooner had it arrived than it vanished, leaving an imprint of worried consternation on the faces of people.

I was called outside to see for myself the liquid droplets of pigeon-blood coloured water that had fallen out of the blue from a cloudless sky.

"O My Child, what big storms are rising," Engrácia said in a voice of bad omens, her eyes staring at the ground.

I tried to rationalise the weirdness of the phenomenon by looking at the clear skies of spring and asking when it had rained and whether anyone had seen the shower.

No, no one had. It had been a stealthy, quick thing. Some people had only realised what had happened because of the strange drops which had been left on the ground and on the grass and on the leaves of plants. Others had only become aware of the occurrence from seeing spattered stones and window panes tarnished with a never-before-seen carmine film.

As best as I could, I tried to calm their spirits, saying it must have been rain coming from the African deserts. I summoned reason with what I thought was the most logical explanation for something I had never seen before. Perhaps nobody would worry if they thought it was rain tinged with the fine sands of the desert.

Of course, no one was convinced, and neither was I. Blood had rained over Nothing, and Engrácia's ill-fated foreboding was a cloud darkening my thoughts as though a storm were gathering in the distance. I told everyone to go back to minding their work and asked the servants to clean the windows.

For days there was talk of the blood rain, until the spring sun had it forgotten and added to the catalogue of the myths of Nothing.

Life went on. It was the time of fruits: Lawson pears, peaches and apricots. Abundance was back in its unyielding cycle.

In the beginning of summer we took a new man into our service. He spoke a musical Portuguese, more out of trial and error than knowledge. He arrived at our gates asking for work and, in the midst of the hustle and bustle of summer crops ready to be harvested and exuberant vegetable gardens where tomatoes and melons got riper by the day, the extra help was welcome for the propping of the vines.

Father frowned at the hiring, but being too busy to listen to him, I added the man to our payroll and asked our administrator to find him a place to sleep.

He was a good worker and entertained people with the Spanish musicality of his words. For a while, his exoticism lent some colour to Nothing.

Father, however, was not convinced.

"Daughter, we have to send the Spaniard away."

"But why, Father? The man hasn't done anything wrong."

"I know, Daughter, but we can't keep him here. It's dangerous ... "

Father was afraid we might be denounced. He was well aware of the fugitives in Barrancos and worried, lest the authorities should come to Nothing to take the Spaniard and arrest us for collaborating with the anti-Francoist resistance by harbouring a revolutionary.

Of course I understood Father but was not willing to yield to his fears and supplications. I knew of the Civil War. I knew Poland had been invaded a few months earlier.

I knew you were fiercely on the loose.

At first I neither noticed him much nor did I single him out from the other workers at Nothing. Father's insistence to have him sent away was the catalyst that made me become more interested in him and realise that, in fact, we were giving shelter, if not to a refugee, at worst a fugitive.

At a time of repression and difficulties, my heart was telling me that compassion was inasmuch a duty as a feeling I was allowed to. Little by little, I started to draw near him when he came back from the vineyards at the end of the day. Engaging in some kind of conversation, I would ask him whether he was adapting well to Nothing.

"Sí, sí, Doña Luísa, muy bien."

Also, I would offer to take him the delicacies and tidbits of our rural cuisine, such as shredded cod salad with paprika and onions, or *pataniscas*, our renowned cod patties, served with a rich risotto of red beans.

No, Ángel was not to go away unless he so wished. My dead emptiness was finding fulfillment in complacency. Besides, although I was unable to verbalise it consciously, that Catalonian man was a sort of catapult bringing me back to life. Maybe those had been selfish purposes which had led me to receive Ángel Aguirre in Nothing.

There was a long row of small, one-storey terraced houses where the workers of Nothing took lodging. Ángel was quartered in the far end of the terrace and by nightfall I would drop in bearing plates covered by dish towels, telling him to enjoy what we cooked so well. With the open smile of someone feeling welcome in the company of strangers, he would say thank you to everything. Sometimes he would even ask me to dine with him, thus sharing the meal I so gladly had taken him. Assenting, I would tell him that I could nibble only a little because I was due at home where my family awaited me for supper. However, I would invariably prolong my visit and listen to the many stories about his country.

Republican, he had fled from Catalonia at the onset of the war. In 1936 he had crossed the Ardila River as part of a refugee contingent which got to the small southern village of Barracos in the Portuguese-Spanish border.

Anti-Francoist dissidents in Portugal were obviously a major diplomatic embarrassment for our regime. On the one hand, there was pressure from the Spanish nationalist army, ready for an invasion to take the refugees back to the country. On the other, our Fascist regime was sympathetic to kindred ideologies and therefore supportive of the *pronunciamento*, the formal declaration, against the government of President Manuel Azaña. Lastly, there was also international pressure not to return the refugees to the pro-Francoist authorities. Trying a compromise solution, we sent them to

Tarragona in Republican Extremadura.

Somehow Ángel managed to escape the forced repatriation and, in a recent and far from pacified post-war, he had not returned to Spain.

He told me he was from Barcelona, a bohemian city of sea and artists, and that he had fled the war the same year it had started. Because of those things, I supposed he was a leftist Republican and, my Father being a staunch Monarchist, I took that to be the main hindrance he saw to Ángel's permanence in Nothing, rather than the fear of someone denouncing us for having a Spaniard working for us and living with us at a time when the presence of unfamiliar Spaniards with unclear pasts was an evident cause for suspicion.

Not once did I intrude on the things he did not tell me about. Politics and his escape were such things. Everything I could possibly know was either inferred or suspected, and most often imagined.

I have no idea what had moved me when I found myself knocking gently at the door that night. In the dark of that September, so similar to all other Septembers when Nothing fell asleep in the tiredness of hot vintage days, I had hastily groped the way I had known for all my life and dared not be stopped in my hurried steps.

I thought about nothing so that I could not give myself the chance for losing courage or last-minute regrets. No one dared be awakened. Stealth and haste were of the essence. I silenced my breath while I was walking in that direction.

Below the wicket, I knocked softly at the clapboard door. The bolt was unfastened and I slipped in, camouflaged by the dark-blue shroud of the night.

There were no words. He was a man, I was a woman and that was primordial.

I know not what possessed me to come to him. Maybe it was the adrenaline of danger or of the enigmatic, unknown man. Or maybe it was the fact that, as a foreigner, he would not linger in my present or in the days of Nothing. I needed him in a hallucinated moment which had overcome my rationality. My desire for a wild experience was sovereign over any reproaches of reason. Besides, there were no reasons. Something in me had wanted that, and I had capitulated without a care for inner moral outcries. After all, what else in life could I possibly lose that I had not already lost?

He kissed me savagely. He threw me, dispossessed, onto the bed. He used me as I used him. If I had come, it was because I had so wanted and, consequently, all was allowed. His muscles, so distinct from the more delicate bodies of the bourgeois men I had known, were tight and strong from intensive toil. He was also more of a man in the sense of being endowed with the disentangled animality of someone used to living permanently on the run. He loved me in ways I had not known to be possible and there were moments when his audacity scared me. But I wanted it all. I wanted to discover everything. If he could teach me, then I kept still in order to learn and let him do to me what best pleased him.

When it was over and I returned to my bedroom, to my house, to my safe bed, I ran my fingers through every place he had touched me. I wanted to know whether I was still the same Luísa or a something else just born out of that encounter. Overflowing with a new pleasure and a novel and different consciousness of me, I touched my warm skin and my body.

Ángel was neither António nor Antero and I was not the Luísa who had become a woman with António and with Antero. I was now a Luísa who belonged solely and totally to Luísa. Former chapters of my life had given me a liberty whose fruits I was now reaping. I wanted to sleep naked and fell asleep with my hands between my bent legs, feeling the soft caress of fresh linen sheets on my skin. The hollow cocoon of my dead soul was experiencing a new pleasure, one exclusively explained by pleasure itself.

I went back to his house in the nights that followed as though I had become addicted to a forbidden, and all the more wanted, substance. Sleep deprivation was a nuisance during the day but the visits to Ángel's bed did not stop. Only the light of the full moon held me back for a brief few days.

The violence of perspiring bodies was balsamic to me. The hard mattress, stuffed with the husks of corn ears, and its crackling, dry sound transmitted the wild side of it all and stood in direct opposition to the high, comfortable bed that awaited me at the other end of my nights.

I paid his wages for the first week of October and the next morning we realised he was gone. Neither did I find it odd nor did I reply to any comments I might have heard about the sudden departure of the Spaniard. To me he was just another anonymous stranger who had gone away from Nothing like so many other seasonal workers. Depending on the cycle of crops, workers came and went, and that was it. It would not be because we had shared one another that I was going to feel anything more special. The end had come soon for something which had not even started. Pleasure for pleasure's sake gives us no bindings of either body or conscience. My freedom was the same as it was before, during or after Ángel's staying among us in Nothing.

Father felt relieved because that man was a Spaniard who had come at a time of doubts and wars, and all that was enough to raise fear.

For my part, I had only one more secret to add to the secrets I seemed to collect without ever having had the intention of making my life a journey of unspeakable, unsharable things. Life had picked me and, bordering my thirties, there was not much I could do to erase my secrets. Neither was I willing to do anything about them. My greater or lesser happiness was not dependent on my secrets. Moreover, happiness was nothing to me.

A fortnight after Ángel's disappearance, when we were no longer reminded of him, two Republican guards from Vila Franca stopped by at the gates of Nothing. They were looking for an Ordoño Güellar, a dangerous Anarchist agitator wanted by the Francoist authorities, who had been seen in the vicinity. They brought a warrant for his capture and a photograph of a disheveled man with the dark stubble of many days that showed a sinister resemblance to Ángel. With the unison voice of complicity, Father and I said we had no idea who that man was, and lucky for us we were the owners of the great Nothing or we would have been further bothered with that matter.

When the police officers left, I could sense that Father's thoughts were on me and the danger we had been in. It was easy to realise he was silently reproaching me for the imprudence of having allowed Ángel to work for us, but I was above his criticism which meant nothing to me. Likewise, I was unperturbed to know the truth about Ángel and that he was not the man we had met. For all I cared, that was a closed chapter and end of the story. It was indifferent whether I had slept with the serene Ángel or the dangerous Ordoño. What mattered was not betraying my determination not to give myself to feelings and emotional prisons, or I would have to face potential hurt and loss again.

With Ángel I had been true to me.

XV

It was not time yet. The excruciating pain awakened me and I struggled down the stairs to ask Engrácia for help. I knew too well what it meant. It could not be happening.

"O My Child, it can't be!" Engrácia cried, pulling herself out of her bed. In the panic of seeing me in such a state, she rushed, still in her nightgown, to wake up the maids, telling them to hurry to Ladeirinhas to get help.

Warm blood mixed with water was running down my legs.

"Engrácia, it can't be!"

I was crying, helplessly. I could not be having the child. It was too soon.

The Spaniard had left me pregnant of unknown father. My child was not going to have a surname other than a surname of Nothing. Of course everybody guessed I was having a child of the Spaniard. No complex conjectures were needed to know that my pregnancy was a result of a misstep.

When I had to deliver the news to Father because my womb was going to grow, his deep sigh carried all the shame and sadness of the betrayal he felt.

I heard him say, "I didn't think you were that..."

In his unfinished sentence, I felt embarrassed and belittled in his eyes.

I did not admonish myself for what I had done with Ángel. I regretted nothing. The pregnancy was all the more wanted for being a pregnancy lived in freedom and without the shackles of the child's father. Nonetheless, seeing the pain in Father's face was like a sting in my heart, for I felt I had let him down. I knew how much he could be hurt by people's tongues, especially now that the tongues would be speaking about me. As always, I cared little about what the loose tongues of people had to say in delight about the fall of others. But Father was incapable of such cold distancing.

For her part, Mother received the news in her usual silence, her eyes staring at the infinite, beyond the sheer curtains that filtered the light coming through the windows and into her room.

Engrácia called me crazy and asked me where my head was, if I realised what I had done and whether I had any notion of what was going to happen to this fatherless child. When her fury subsided, she came to a grieving state that pitied my strange destiny.

"O, the fate of this Child of Mine; another child on the way without a father. By God, what sad fate."

Obviously, I was not in the least fond of that lament, because I did not see myself under a prism of sorrow. I had wanted to lie down with that man, and I wanted this child. Damn, everyone was looking forward for an heir to Nothing. Couldn't they just be happy because it was going to happen?

After the rage, the sighs, the pitying, there came the happier feelings I had been waiting for. Father accepted the fact that, once again, I was going to have a child without having a man. This time around, not even a pseudo-widowhood justified my state. I was a disgraced, single mother. But against facts there could be no arguments, and Nothing would never let me fall into the mud of misery and the commiseration of strangers.

Engrácia, now the epitome of joy, started to prepare the clothes and bedding for the new baby that was coming.

Nothing was said about my son António. There was nothing left of him other than in the memories we tried to keep below the surface of our thoughts. Everything he had been was in a vacuum hermetically shut with bricks and mortar, impossible to open. A new baby was being born into Nothing, and everything had to be ready to welcome it.

For a while my death left me, and I felt a good mood filling my chest. Perhaps my past of losses was bidding its farewell to me. Maybe happiness would still give me a chance. It could be that the impromptu arrival of the Spaniard meant the salvation of Nothing and the deliverance from my pain.

It was possible that I was learning a lesson: Happiness could well be possible even if it came through unexpected and winding ways. Maybe I really was learning that we should not close our hearts because they will always find a way to be opened.

Or, I was being punished for having given myself to pain with promises of not loving again, no matter whom, no matter what. A new child was coming and that could only mean the collapse of all barriers I had erected against love. It served me right. Who had told me to dare not give into love for fear of hurting again?

A child was coming and I was going to love it as though it were my first.

But now? This could not be happening. It could not. Six months pregnant, I could not be dead-birthing this baby. My child had died inside of me and I could not believe I had to go through that. That would not be a punishment; it would be a Machiavellian injustice. Some vindictive or jealous force had cursed me. I felt myself being drained of my blood, and death, sweet death, seemed to be beckoning as strength left me.

I wished for you so much in that hour.

I wanted to die. I wanted so much to die.

The midwife from Ladeirinhas pushed my belly to pull the child out of me. Engrácia wept and screamed for help to all the saints she could name, while begging me not to die.

And I knew I was not going to hear a baby cry at the end of it all. I had to deliver to bury.

I had no wish to see the bundle of soft lace blankets. It was not the same warm and alive bundle that had been António. I could not bring myself to see another dead child.

"It's a girl," said Engrácia in the gentlest of voices, while holding the bundle of lifeless baby in her arms with the same motherly love she had held my other, now dead child and used to hold me.

I turned my head to the window through which the sun of that early March morning was coming, and I used Mother's eyes to look into the distance. Staring without seeing, all of me was a pain insensitive to the outside of me.

"She is so beautiful, My Child. And so perfect . . . " whispered

Engrácia, laying her in the cradle that had meantime been brought to my bedroom. A cradle which was not supposed to be there for another three months.

Engrácia left, leaving me alone with that tiny body taken lifeless from me. The silence around me was a dead silence, and my eyes stared at the light dimmed by the curtain at the window.

I cannot understand why you put me through that. What harm have my children done to you so you had them pulled away from within me with such brutality? And I? What have I done to you? Did you envy me for the men who shared my body? Were you jealous of my freedom to sleep with them without giving into the conventions that would smother me? I hated you for sparing me to the physical end of me.

I died in my soul more than anyone can die in body. For some time I had let myself be deceived into thinking that a part of me could resurrect. But, after all, I had always been dead and, therefore, I could not possibly bear a child to join the world of the living. The dead do not have children.

Numb in every piece of me, I made a superhuman effort to get up from the bed and went to see her.

So small. So little. She was blonde, and Engrácia was right when she said the baby was beautiful and that she was so perfect for her lack of time.

I had a daughter just like me, just like us in Nothing. She seemed to be asleep, and I could not muster the courage to open and look at her eyes. I wanted neither to wake her nor desacralise my memory of her in that peaceful quietude of sleep.

I held her, hugging her in an embrace that would have to last me for a lifetime. An embrace which would be my whole relationship with her. I cried, holding her and missing the warmth I had not known in her. In my thoughts I told her I loved her and asked her to forgive me for having conceived her.

"My daughter, my lovely daughter whom I have never met."

When Father came into the bedroom, I asked him to write Bela Flor[36] on the death certificate and to put her in a white urn like her

---

36. Literally, Beautiful Flower.

brother's. I also asked that the urn be placed on the floor of the vault, under the bottom shelf on the side allotted to my dead. I could not bear to think of her exposed in full view, because she had never really come into this life. I wanted her sheltered in a forgotten corner, she who had not wanted to live for us or meet us.

Convalescing from labour and too weak to stand another funeral of a child of mine, I did not attend the funeral. Later Engrácia would tell me that Mother put on such a thick veil and covered herself in such deep black that not even Death would resemble her. I think that was her way of hiding a pain which, like mine, was consuming the womb known only to maternity.

She stood proud and tall, as tall and proud as was Nothing, and the tongues of the people were silent.

XVI

What has no meaning is what most desperately needs meaning. Once more, mourning took up residence in Nothing, and that mourning needed a culprit, something to exorcise our pain and inability to understand what had happened.

Engrácia, in her need for answers, found the monster which had taken my daughter from us.

It had been pouring. A cold, heavy rain, unlike anything people could remember. The wind hissed ferociously through door cracks and the bare branches of trees. The day had dawned frowning, displeased and angry at the world, growling and vomiting driveling, sloppy furies.

In the coops, the feathered creatures hid their heads beneath their wings and waited patiently for the bad weather to go away. The dogs and the cats of Nothing did not dare to venture away from the porch. Neither were they willing to leave the cosy proximity of the kitchen's stove.

The stables were eerily quiet, and we had no choice but to endure the grey day under the light of electricity, consoled by the popping warmth of the flames burning in the fireplace. It was another of those winter days to endure, somewhat apprehensive of the diluvial downpour, a bit unusual in its vehemence, one might add.

February 15, 1941: The day when even you sought refuge because the monster was on the loose, and it was stronger than you, everything more than you.

The dusky hue of the day made it difficult to discern the exact hour, but it was around noon. All of a sudden the dogs started to howl. I was in the kitchen having some coffee, or, more accurately, a substitute made of roasted, ground barley, which was one of the few things my nauseated pregnancies actually enjoyed.

No matter how hard we tried, there was no silencing the dogs.

Their tense bodies and eyes bright with something we could not identify gave me the unexplained impulse to grab my waxed jacket and go outside to learn what was upsetting the animals so badly.

"Something's coming, Engrácia!," I called, as I hastily pulled my arms into the heavy, cold jacket, while Engrácia and the other maids who were in the kitchen looked on, their faces full of fear.

"Child of Mine, where are you going? You can't go out in this weather. Stay here," Engrácia commanded.

But I barely listened. I was in a hurry to check whether the stables and the cellar were locked tight. I doubted anyone had secured the bolts in anticipation of such a harsh wind. Contributing to my uneasiness, I further suspected there might be open gates and doors that would be posing a threat to our livestock, the hay, the wine.

Stepping out of the kitchen and onto the porch, I looked south, and there it was. I was struck with terror. A thick wall of lead filled the horizon in front of us, overwhelming me by its gigantic proportions. I ran to the cellar before the mountain of water fell over us. The deluge of the Apocalypse was headed in our direction, and it was coming fast.

"Child! Child!," Engrácia shouted from the porch. She too was watching the sky, pregnant with danger. "Child!"

Her screams were suffocated by the raging roar of a strength-gathering wind.

I braved the violence of the gale to get to the wine cellar. The hood of the jacket flew away from my head. My face was beaten with rough, swift flying debris that raked my skin: twigs, leaves, grit.

As I feared, the doors of the cellar were wide open, swinging and banging desolately against the wall. Inside, whirlwinds of hay tangled my hair and made the sharp tools, hanging from the beams that held the roof tiles, dance menacingly above my head. I shut the door against the wind with all the strength my six-month bump allowed me to summon under those circumstances.

That was when the monster, with a snarl of vicious blasts, blew the roof away.

Ducking and turning sharply to avoid the rubble bombarding me, I fell helplessly to the floor.

In the midst of my concern over the cellar and the wine, I did not think about whether I was hurt or not. There was no time to notice myself or my welfare. The world was upside down. All around me the cellar was quaking.

I knew I had to get away from there, head back to the house. Soaking wet and covered in mud, I managed to get up. Two hens flew by. Projectiles. I realised the chicken coop must have been destroyed. Reeds coming from afar, from river banks which had not been cleaned during summer, were added to the dirt the diabolical wind was carrying.

Determined, I ran, trying to dodge the dangerous things that were carried by those strong air currents.

Never have I forgotten the roar of the wind. The Adamastor[37] had been unleashed from whatever cage in which he had been imprisoned for centuries on end. The sudden freedom had given him the rage that he was shacklessly spewing.

On my way to the house, I managed to reach the stable where the horses were neighing, desperate to be set free. Panic made it difficult for me to decide whether it was better to keep them inside, despite the risk of the roof falling down and harming them, or set them free to face the severity of the storm.

My heart was about to burst, so strongly it pounded. Not knowing what to do, I locked myself in the stable, and in a split second made the decision. If the wind took the tiles, I would let the horses go that instant.

Safe behind those stable walls, I could hear the menacing growl outside. Everything was shaking. The roof tiles wobbled, on the brink of detaching themselves like paper sheets from the beams of the roof. I heard the cries and howls of animals outside the stable. I imagined my dogs hurt. The horses kept neighing, wanting to escape. Those moments of anxiety seemed to last forever.

---

37. Adamastor is the mythical giant said to live at the end of the Cape of Good Hope, which, because of its dangerous water currents and winds, was called by Portuguese sailors of the sixteenth century the Cape of Storms. The Adamastor is depicted as the giant opposing Portuguese efforts to reach India by sea in the Portuguese epic The *Lusiad* (1572) by Luiz de Camoens.

Then, gradually, the wind began to abate. Still fearing for the horses, I went to each one, patting and gently whispering that everything was alright. The yoke of oxen that shared the stable with the horses also began to calm down, having endured the storm pouncing against the planks of their enclosure.

When I emerged, the end of the world was before me. Apocalypse had swept the land. The cellar was roofless. The rain, drenching the casks and barrels, could only ruin our wine, the wine of Nothing, which cost us so much work and dedication, year in, year out.

A dead pigeon was lying on the ground at my feet, midst piles of debris of indiscernible things. Stunned chickens and Muscovy ducks wandered, lost, in the yard. The male peacock was calling for its missing mate, and the anguished cry was heartbreaking.

Indeed, the female peacock was never to be found. Later, Father bought a new one so we could obliterate from Nothing all reminders of that dreadful day and not prolong the widowerhood of the forlorn peacock, which reminded Mother of India.

A drooping turkey, looking perplexed and unaware of how it had gotten there, was perched on a branch of the loquat tree.

All around was desolation, chaos and mess.

I got home and found Engrácia tying a cloth around the bloody head of one of the maids who had been in the kitchen. The violence of the wind had torn the chimney down, and the girl had been hit by a shard of collapsing brick. Our kitchen looked as though it had been struck by an earthquake.

I went looking for Father and found him in Mother's room.

That he had gone to her caused me to realise how much he loved her. In the fright of that day, it had been to her that he had turned. It was with her he had wanted to be, and it was her he wanted to protect from the brutal storm which had ravaged us.

Both had the same empty, panic-stricken gaze, as if their entire life had passed in front of their eyes before their ultimate end.

Seeing me dishevelled and tattered, Mother pulled out a handkerchief to wipe my face, where multiple scratches were beginning to sting as I started to regain consciousness of me.

Not used to that kind of intimacy with my Mother and feeling uncomfortable having interrupted a private moment between her and Father, I thanked her and immediately left the room.

I hastened to check the rest of the house, to make sure everything was intact, and then headed back to the kitchen where my presence was needed. It was there the storm had caused the greatest damage.

There was much to rebuild, much to salvage.

The hurricane swept through the whole of Portugal that day. The destruction was incalculable. People died, cars were blown away, electric and telegraph cables were wrecked. Even Lisbon was not spared from the tempest and, as I later discovered while going through the clippings Mother kept of that day, there was no memory of such a terrible storm. Forever, that fateful 15 February 1941 was deemed the day of the hurricane.

To justify the unjustifiable, Engrácia credited the wind monster with my child born dead two weeks later. Maybe the stress of that day, my fall in front of the cellar, the shock from all the destruction, or the scare, had contributed to what happened afterwards. I do not know. I lost my daughter before she was born and that was a monster of death far more horrendous than the hurricane. My fertile womb was birthing holocaust offerings, beings immolated before my very own eyes without my being able to rescue them. Never was I allowed to be the mother who saves her children inasmuch as I was not the mother who raises children. I had them only to be taken away from me and so death could receive them early in life. I died and wished to die of a deadlier death than the one I lived. And that is why I have never been able to locate the exact moment when I really died.

XVII

The new great war that had settled in was felt mostly in the rationing. In Nothing we exchanged chickens and olive oil for the coffee and sugar coupons of the people coming here searching for the things they lacked. We had always been self-sufficient but, of course, we grew neither coffee nor cocoa. We were also not very keen on butter making and therefore we felt its being rationed.

In Vila Franca, the houses which did not have a vegetable garden or a piece of land were struggling with the shortage in food supplies, and a lot of people came to our door looking for provisions. In those times of want, we accepted that people gave us their sugar or coffee coupons — the rationing tickets, as the government called them — as barter for more essential and perishable goods such as poultry or milk. We had no need for so many coffee coupons, but we took them as payment for the produce we dispensed. It was a sort of camouflaged charity so as not to hurt the pride of people who wanted to pay us and had no other means to than coupons. After all, Salazar had promised to save us from the war but not from famine. We never used all the coupons we were given and, if I go through my account books for that period, I will still find a few of them.

We also had to hide things from the State's inspectors. Olive oil was probably the most sought after, most rationed, most hidden and most smuggled product. We filled large vessels with the year's oil that we then concealed beneath the trapdoors in the stables. In 1943, when we still had no idea how much longer the war would last, they created the General Supplies Administration,[38] the infamous government agency responsible for supervising the rationing of food

---

38. In Portuguese, IGA, Intendência Geral dos Abastecimentos. Created in 1943, IGA was devised to supervise, control and implement the rationing of food supplies that resulted from the shortages brought about by the impact of the War on the Portuguese economy. As a central State agency, it had the duty of imposing sanctions on rationing violations. Because the IGA was closely associated with the *Estado Novo*, the population usually looked upon it with suspicion.

and, worse than that, enforcing sanctions on violators. It was that aspect of State intrusion and control that was particularly upsetting to us. Indeed, we never had any political troubles but, because we were a house of plenty, the GSA had its eye on us. They wanted a percentage of what we produced. Hiding the barrels of olive oil prevented their confiscating it.

Cash was another rare commodity. Many times I went to Vila Franca carrying gold sovereigns in my pockets to buy the things we needed in Nothing. I would buy in bulk and exchange a sovereign for the provisions I acquired. From the past of us, we had inherited from our ancestors a wood bushel box containing a small treasure of gold coins. To it I would turn each time I needed to shop. I would go to the little pile, take a coin, and off I went. More often than not I paid far too much. Naturally, some flour and a few pieces of salted cod would never be as expensive as a gold sovereign, but such were the times. Better to have the flour and the cod than gold trapped in a box.

We lived in a constant fear of another La Lys that might take one of ours from us. Many times I found myself thinking about Uncle Romano. And I believe Father must have also, and way more than I did. However and fortunately, the most that happened to us was one or another boy from Ladeirinhas was drafted to the Azores, where our expeditionary forces were stationed in the event of hostilities. The radio connected us to a daunting and grim world, and although the war of machine guns and battle fronts was not hitting us directly, we felt that Nothing was partaking in that era of war and death. The hurricane, my dead daughter, everything made us share the horrors which millions were suffering.

The forties were gruesome in Nothing. After the foreshadowing blood rain, there came the hurricane and, from 1943 onwards, a succession of consecutive dry years took a toll on our fields before the drought reached a climax near the turn of the decade, in 1948 to 1949. We fought as best as we could. We built a dam in the stream and had dowsers sent in to dig new wells. We recycled and saved water, very much aware of not wasting it. But out on the fields, in the vineyards and orchards there was not much we could do.

Father kept withering by the day. Like my Grandfather Américo, he started to look for the west-facing wall of the house where he could sit and let the winter sun warm his body. The sadness of my life's events weakened him, and for that reason I could not completely indulge in the death I was living. His life mattered to me more than my death, and Nothing needed reins so as not to regress into wilderness by setting it loose from the iron domestication under which we kept it. Even when the agricultural years were bad, there was no break in the toil and labour the immense farm required. I had cried for my son in the maritime recess of Ericeira, but the herculean pains of Nothing and the love for Father were obstacles preventing me from having the peace and quiet to mourn my daughter. I was not allowed the time to feel the pain that pain deserved. However, what good was there in crying the pain of death when I had died so long ago?

Do you cry yourself out for you? I do not think so.

Why should I stray further and further away from the grief within me when I had been living in grief ever since the moment they took António lifeless from the still lake while I was still in mourning for Grandfather?

I took Father to the doctor in Vila Franca when I realised his lack of vigour was more than the sadness inflicted by my sorrows. I got him in the car and drove him to the practice of Doctor D'Além, the most famed and respected physician around. The diagnosis was merciless.

A bad tumour.

Father had a bad tumour. In his prudish shame, Father had never told me about a cyst growing under his armpit and that, lately, a watery liquid was coming out of it.

I was mad at him for not having told me anything. Mad that he always wanted to be so strong in my eyes. Mad he had hidden that from me. I was seeing red when I drove us back to Nothing on that hapless afternoon after the doctor's appointment.

"But why, Father? How long have you had that thing there? Did I have to find out you're not well to know you have that?"

I grilled him with a hundred questions, as if he were the one to blame for that news, he who was the victim.

Anger was the first and only reaction I had. It was the way my mind, my heart and my body were finding to cope with the terrible thing I had heard the doctor say after he had seen Father and asked to have a word in private with me. How was it possible that my Father had a tumour? A cancer chewing him from the inside?

Sleep did not find me that night as I laid countless plans in my mind to save my Father. My Father.

I kept repeating "my Father" over and over again to make myself aware that what was happening involved my Father, the person I loved the most in this life. My rod and my staff, my strength. My immortal being without whose existence I could not imagine my own and Nothing's. My Father.

The next morning, it was not at Father that I was furious. It was at me; it was at everything.

Father, I reckoned in absolute certainty, must have become ill about the time I lost the baby and had not told me anything so as not to add to my suffering. Meantime, a whole year had passed with his getting worse and still not telling me anything. It was all because of me and all the maladies I brought to this family. It was because of the wicked hurricane that kept me busy in reconstruction work to make Nothing get back to being Nothing again. And it was because of Mother who would not care less whether he was well or not. My poor Father, so harassed by us and yet so careful in not giving us the slightest reason to fret over him.

My dear, adored Father was ill.

Father's treatment was set to start immediately, as I was not going to tolerate a single second of delays. Taking the letters and prescriptions from Doctor D'Além, I hurried to Lisbon, where Father was to be hospitalised at Capuchos, the hospital of Saint Anthony of the Capuchin Order, and rented a house nearby, so as to be close to him. During my absence, and in the face of Mother's complete uselessness for minding the affairs of the farm, Nothing was left in the hands of our administrator and Engrácia.

When Father came out of the hospital, two weeks after the surgery that removed his tumour, I remained with him in Lisbon. I wanted him to convalesce within the reach of doctors and hospitals, not in the far-off exile of Nothing. A nurse was hired and Father was to be provided with all comforts and care. His recovery and well-being were my sole purpose in life.

I wrote to Mother once a week but never gave any hint that her presence was required. In those letters, I only told her about the progress of the treatments, the opinions of the doctors or other minor details, such as Father eating well, or, on the contrary, being unable to muster an appetite. Unlike her, who had written me that letter during my retreat in Ericeira, a letter that was all meaning, all distance, yet, paradoxically, infinite intimacy, I did not find it in me to write to her that way. Feelings were something I was not used to sharing with her. I even feared the letters on the paper. I feared they made me write things I did not want, things like how afraid I was of the outcome of the treatments or the excruciating pain that ravaged my body in seeing my Father subjected to such an ordeal.

Never did I let Mother know of my filial humanity. Never did I tell her how I loved Father with every fiber of me. That Father had taught me everything I knew, taught me the love she had never shown me and that, therefore, was impossible to be inherited or learnt from her. Of course she was more than aware of the insurmountable difference in feelings I nurtured for her and for Father and of the unbreakable links connecting me to that loving man of warm hands. As such, what was there to write about in those letters that she did not already know?

I was scared of the words that might come out of me and onto the paper far more because I feared me than because I was afraid of exposing myself to Mother or overcoming the coldness that characterised our so formal relationship. Reading what came from within the deepest of me in relation to my horror of losing Father meant opening a sore wound and treating it with salt. My dead children were a chronic pain. Father's illness was a pain which made me dread the future. The possibility of losing him was so overwhelming an anguish that I was afraid of any kind of words that might make me face it.

Throughout the month Father and I spent in Lisbon, Mother never showed up and I did not miss her.

In the afternoons when he felt strong enough, we would go to Rossio to have some refreshments. During the day I let him have his quiet, sitting by the tall shutters opening to a magnificent view of the Castle over the canopy of the jacaranda trees that lined the street. His rural soul, however, longed for Nothing. Many were the times he begged me to take him back, saying he was cured and there was no need to be there, wasting time in a town that meant nothing to him.

With the doctors' agreement I took him home.

The return was good for him. The scar had healed and the discomfort of an infected tumour was gone. Even his cheeks, haggard from the domesticated air of the city, regained some colour. And his eyes, my God, his velvety eyes shone with the freedom of being away from the cage whose embodiment was that wood-floored apartment with vases of orange geraniums whose roots were trapped by the baked clay. I had my Father back.

The great Nothing would restore his health.

As he could not ride, lest it strain his arm fresh from surgery, we went for long walks on the gravel paths of the vast fields of Nothing. We made plans: ditches in want of cleaning, the deep furrows that needed to be dug in the Cruz vineyard in order to air the roots of the vines and manure them, and so many other things.

Summer came and with it the most exuberant period in the calendar of Nothing. I held Father's arm and felt snuggled in that physical proximity with my own blood. Father was back.

Comforting thoughts anticipated vintage, the hustle and bustle of the people in the vineyards and in the cellars, the new wine in the barrels. We had struggled against the beast, and we had vanquished. All the labour of Nothing was our rewarding rest. We were happy in the sweet wait of the days of arduous toil ahead. Holding Father's arm, Nothing warmed my heart. I smiled in those times. Of everything I had already lost, I had not lost Father.

My Father.

XVIII

"My Child, come with me to the kitchen."

Engrácia had come looking for me in the pantry-office. In a gentle, low voice she was asking me to follow her into the kitchen. She had something to show me.

It was September. I was busy with the thousand and one things critical to the beginning of vintage. The people we had to hire, the cellars, and the implements: buckets, baskets, vats, scissors, saccharometers. The red and the white wine, the vineyards of table grapes and the middlemen who took them to the markets in Vila Franca and Lisbon. The order by which we started vintage: first in the vineyards facing west, where grapes matured earlier, then the ones to the east. Assigning the workers and making sure all containers, buckets and scissors were washed at the end of the day so the sticky, sweet juice of the grapes would not sour the harvest of the following day. All of those concerns took up my days, to the infinitesimal second, from dawn to way past dusk. However seasoned I was by years of experience, the intensity of work did not allow for major breaks. So I did not pay much attention to whatever it was Engrácia wanted from me.

"Anita's just brought these in from Daddy's bedroom," she said, showing me the sheets where a huge irregular-shaped, yellowy stain of brownish contours forecast our future. Pus.

My heart shuddered as if a dagger had pierced through it. The beast was back.

I ran for Father, frightened and knowing the battle was about to start all over again. With each step, I felt strength forsaking me, leaving me in desperate, hopeless hope. I found him in the cellar talking to our administrator. I called him aside. Vintage was over for me. Now only Father filled my thoughts, my worries, my heart.

"I know about the sheets, Father. We are going to Doctor D'Além straight away." I struggled to summon maximum determination from the midst of my panic.

"That's nothing, Daughter. It's probably just a suture that opened," he replied, knowing I knew he lied.

"The sutures are healed, Father. We're going to Doctor D'Além. Now. Come, let's go".

With my head, I beckoned him to come. From the strength I lacked, I made myself strong for that moment. I made my voice utter the certainty that it was probably something irrelevant and only required attention in order not to grow in importance. Pretending not to be scared, I assured him everything would be alright; it was no big thing, but we had to see to it immediately. I held the reins as though I were the strongest person on the face of the earth.

"Luísa, don't do that to me. Can't you see I don't want any more doctors?"

The sincerity of his grief-stricken request broke my heart. I could feel it being torn apart into tiny bits so as to hurt me more. Nothing hurts more in life than the hurt of those we love. My own pains were nothing by comparison to the pain of seeing my Father ill, of listening to the pain in his voice. A thousand times would I die for him and none would cause me suffering. A thousand times would I barter my life of nothing to have him spared any vestige of harm. Everything. Everything would I give, everything would I trade, I would immolate myself if that would rescue my Father from pain.

"But you must, Daddy. Please, let's go to Doctor D'Além," I implored.

I foresaw what was ahead of us, the devastating fight that would drain us of our strength, that would ache us in every fiber. There it was and I could not get away from it, let alone allow that Father, no matter how tired he was, could get away from it. Together we would face it. We had to save him, and I was going to save him with or without his agreement. I was the adult in that equation of us. I was the generation coming of age. I was the daughter whose time had come to take care of her parents. Yes, the time to look after the parents was there and my Father needed me just as I had always, and always, needed him and always would. There could be no delaying. Urgency was of the essence.

I forced him. I cannot say I convinced him to come with me to the doctor.

He resigned himself to my obliging him. He gave in only not to hurt me. Everything that followed was against his will, and yet he endured it all for the love of me and because I said so and that was the right way to go.

My poor, beloved Father.

Again we were engrossed in fighting the bad tumour which had resurrected, now more aggressive than before.

We took him back to the hospital at Capuchos, where he underwent surgery again. This time, however, the sutures were not healing, and he was withering before my eyes on that narrow hospital bed.

The doctors came to me to have the talk I could not tolerate. They told me to prepare, that it was unlikely the tumour could regress. I could take my Father home and give him peace and comforting in the stage that followed.

The stage that followed...

How could I accept something like that? No, I did not have to prepare. I did not have to accept any bloody next phase. I knew far too well what kind of phase the doctors meant. Stupid euphemism to refer to my Father's last days. All I had to do was fight. In my heart was the iron impossibility to reject hope.

Hope offered me no peace for what had to be, and today I concede that hope is a failed invention. Hope blinds us and gives us the superhuman strength of madness, of non-acceptance, of non-conformity, the strength that exhausts us. Hope wears us out. Because of it, we do not stop, we do not defer to any voice other than its voice.

I had to have hope because that was the only way for me not to succumb to despair on the journey to save the Father I loved so dearly. Hope gave me the strength that drained me.

After the doctors, I scoured the land for healers and sorcerers and took Father to all sorts of miracle makers. I had waters brought in from special fountains. I made promises in the faith I never had. I prayed to unknown saints and to a God who had never spared me. I wore Father out trying to wear out his illness and refused to yield to his wishes to be left in peace. I moved mountains and spent the rivers of money that Nothing had saved throughout the generations. Nothing was too expensive or too innovative or too strange to save Father. There was no doctor I did not seek, nor second or third or fourth opinion for which I did not ask. Father's illness became my life, my daily job, my reason to exist and my love's Calvary. There was nothing besides or beyond that tumour. There was nothing besides or beyond Father, not even Nothing.

Until there was a day when the quest ceased. The inevitable had come to tell me that from now on it was in charge.

Father was going away from this life. One day he could not get out of bed. Another day he was unable to sit. And another, he could barely eat. Each day he died a little. I cannot describe what it is to say goodbye in installments. To bid farewell to that man a bit more each day was a daily mutilation of my heart. With each part of him that was irretrievably lost, another piece of me was stripped from me in cold blood. I cannot fathom how, in my living death, I could die more and more each day, as if I were infinite, and equally infinite the possibilities of pain.

I started to sleep in his bedroom so I could hold on to each moment I still had with him. Oftentimes, I touched his hands to feel the warmth coming from him that would have to serve me as a memory. I tried to gather as many memories as possible. Totally aware of that goodbye, I arranged everything so as to be next to him as much as possible. I kissed his forehead, tucked his bedclothes.

Mine was a constant vigil so he was not alone in your presence.

One day he woke up from his nap and, with his arm emaciated by the nearing end and by the corrosion of disease, beckoned me to come closer to him, and where he lay in bed. His breath was laboured, the difficult inhale and exhale louder than his own voice.

"Daughter, take care of your Mother. Love her. Forgive her her ways. Hold no grudges. Promise, Daughter. Promise me that."

His eyes told me more than his voice, for they were connected to his all-feeling heart. Wide in the middle of his thinned face, they looked bigger, sadder than the eyes I had known for an entire life.

At that moment, I found them so reminiscent of Uncle Romano's eyes in the sorrow they harboured.

"I promise, Father," I replied, caressing his hand.

I promised him and because of him. Although my heart did not believe that promise, I promised hard. I made Father believe my answer was sincere because I wanted it to be sincere, because I had to be sincere.

On hearing my reply, he looked at me with the deep eyes of his soul and nodded his head. The nod that said he believed me. These were my Father's last words. His will. His final wish. Father was saying goodbye to life while securing Mother's.

He did not wake up the following day. His breath was serene, his eyes half-closed. We tried to feed him some puree but he no longer knew how to swallow.

I begged him not to die. I promised him he would be better. My words urged him to have hope, the mad hope to which I was clinging tenaciously, the hope that was mine and mine alone, but he had forsaken long ago. I asked him to wake up.

Only Mother seemed to understand him. Seeing him leave and being unable to do anything to keep him here led me to despair. But she would come into the room in an astounding calmness of spirit, sit on the bedside and stroke his hair. She did not speak, and her silence soothed his heavy breathing. Then she would leave, and I would remain in the room with all the words that needed to come out of me, to beg him.

"Stay with me, Father. Stay with me."

I lost my shame of crying in front of him. I stopped feeling awkward for having let him see my weakness.

"Daddy, don't go away. Please, Daddy."

For a week I begged and begged and thus kept him artificially alive with my pleading. As always, he obeyed me, out of love. Just as he had relinquished his own will without a complaint for a second wave of treatments, he held back death to make me happy, to grant my filial wishes. And each time Mother entered the room, I could read in the glances she threw at me that she wanted me to stop it.

One day I unexpectedly met her in the corridor. She had been with him and I was coming from the kitchen with a bowl of watery broth to give him with a teaspoon.

I insulted her.

"You're cold! Cold! You never cared for him."

In my unbridled rage I did not give her the opportunity to retort or defend herself.

I imagine her silence was the answer. The bile that sounded so bitter and harsh in my words must have hurt her like arrows. Regret has led me to thinking about it, but at the time I had only one single pain: the open sore in my heart for the life ending there before my eyes. The life that meant everything to me.

I fought you hard and you had a difficult time taking him from me. Or maybe he defeated you by keeping you waiting until he left after we said goodbye. And only then.

At the end of that week, by far the most tortured and anguished of my life, I realised my selfishness. No matter how often I called Mother "cold", she was right. That was no life for Father. I could not say I loved him and then subject him to that. He did not deserve that suspended existence between here and there.

XIX

It was six in the afternoon of a day in September 1943.

I entered the room where the mourning of living death was progressing. Nearing the bed, I stroked the face crisscrossed by the trails of his life. I know not how I mustered the words, how I let them out. Words that scared me, for they were words of absolute and ultimate ending. Words locked in a dungeon in the deepest and darkest recess within me.

"Dearest Daddy, don't stay here. Don't wait any longer. We're going to be alright, Daddy. Never look back. Don't come back here. Set yourself free, Father. Set yourself free. . . . If you see me crying, don't be sad. It's normal." My words were a mere murmur, my every muscle shivering from the violence to which I submitted them in that final but necessary, painful farewell.

"I love you so much, Daddy. . . ." I leaned over him and kissed his forehead, wetting it with the unbound, flowing tears I could not hold back. "My dear Father, don't stay here, because I'll be alright, Mother will be alright."

I wished for eloquent words for the moment, but all I had were the simple, colloquial words of the language I had shared with him for a lifetime. I wanted to be cultured and refined, but I was merely human. I wanted to put his mind at ease, assure him that he should not be concerned about the responsibilities and worries that kept him here. But all I could tell him was that we would be alright, whatever that would mean. I wanted to give him a magnificent epitaph that he might still hear, but I failed. That was my Father lying there, my Father. And I, who wanted nothing but to honour him, was able to say only meaningless things, using trivial words.

He died when I could no longer make words come out of me. He died in my arms, wetted by my tears. I cried because my body and soul wanted to cry. This was not the pain of losing a child, the excruciating pain of torn womb. This was the caring pain of a long love of years and seasons. The natural pain of a child losing a parent, the pain of orphanhood that follows generations after generations. I said goodbye to my Father in my arms and they took him to the other side.

I gave him to you, and I saw you receive him in love. You took him from my arms and we both lulled him, as we would a child, wrapping him in velvet and dignity. That man was now going to light up some other dimension. You came looking for him because you missed him and I had already had him long enough to know his light and his love. I understood you. I understood you with such clairvoyance that I needed not verbalise the thought. I acquiesced.

I remained at his side until the sinking sunlight grayed the afternoon, until I felt he was beginning to lose his warmth and I knew he was no longer there. Slowly, I got up, my tears dry.

I had news to deliver to Nothing. Enveloped in calm composure, I announced the not unexpected outcome.

I asked that the bells toll for a deceased of Nothing and gave orders to prepare the funeral. I had the vault filled with fresh flowers from the gardens of Nothing, prepared his Sunday suit and brushed the felt hat that was to be placed by his hands during the vigil service.

Mother knew he had died before I did. When I went into her room, she put her hand out to me and, opening her closed palm, showed me Grandfather Américo's gold cufflinks. I saw where the force of her grip had left biting marks on her flesh. There was no need to tell her anything.

On my Father's death, there was only a sentence between my Mother and me.

"Grandfather would want him to wear these," she told me softly, handing me the cufflinks.

Then she turned toward the window, her distant gaze looking beyond the endless horizon. I cannot imagine what her eyes saw, but whatever it was it was not in this terrestrial, corporal existence I sensed she was speaking to Father and, likewise, something in me said he was listening. Now that he was rid of that lifeless body, he could hear and see again.

We buried Manel from Nothing with the solemn honor we owed him. We added him to the Boshoff.

Stories and episodes were told about him. Things I did not know that involved his laughter, his spontaneity, his generosity. I received love from the people because their love was devoted to him.

I was gladdened because, in his death, I knew more about him. And I knew he was cherished. As always, it was not from Mother I heard these things. It was not Mother who let me know more about Father. What I was hearing came from the people. The people who had talked about Margarida and Uncle Romano and Mother. The people who had pitied my fate and gloated over my missteps; those people dignified my Father. The people employed by Nothing held a genuine respect for Father, one that had not been imposed by his position as master of Nothing. My Father had been a light, and it was as light that they talked about him. My Father had been a simple man, a man of uncomplicated affections, a trustworthy man of righteousness, and the simple folk anointed him with the simplicity of their words about him.

For me, there were never more sanctified words than those. I was filled with an immeasurable pride for being his daughter and could almost forget the many worries I had given him. Wishing I had not let him down so much, I would have liked to have known whether something in my life had made me him proud. But I knew I was a good daughter. Above all, I knew how much I loved him and was sure he knew it.

The pain of my Father's death was different. I lived it in peace. That is to say I lived it with my heart at ease and free from anger. Father had known I loved him. I knew and felt I had been loved by him. Together we had trodden life and tilled Nothing. He had always been there for me and I had always been there for him. My relationship with him had had neither bumps nor regrets. A final end could be written.

I was now keeper of Nothing.

XX

After Father died, I realised the meaning of my coming to this Earth: I had not come to multiply; I had come to accompany mine to their final Golgotha. I had come to be the middle woman between here and there. I had come so they would not leave in loneliness, so they could have the vault neat and ready to welcome them. I had come to take care of, not transmit myself to others. After Father's departure I knew, with the certainty of absolute unavoidability, that I would bury Mother, and I accepted the commission.

I accepted for myself the loneliness I feel in you.

Every day I am reminded of him. At every second he is somewhere in a part of me: conscious memories or moods of the heart which go by unattended albeit my knowing they are there. The remembrance of him pains me for being happy. It hurts me, the loss of that person, that warming presence which accompanied my days. The amputation is what hurts me, not his death. It is a pain I welcome as good and which hurts, but not without my understanding why it hurts. I know its reason and I do not rebel against it. I have resigned myself to his physical death and his absence from Nothing.

In the days and weeks immediately following his death, however, I purged the suffering of my fresh mourning by attacking Mother ferociously. I blamed her for never having been tender and loving. I accused her of not having loved Father, of not having made him a happy man, a whole man. I judged her. I assumed her to be my responsibility solely because she was my parent, and I granted her no esteem. To all my ire she responded with silence, living, as usual, between her bedroom and her small sitting-room with its bookcase carved into the wall.

Widowhood changed neither her ways nor her routines. Never did she tell me what she felt for Father or whether he was in her memory, as he was in mine, at each and every instant. The same way, she never told me if she had fallen in love with him. Not once did she share with me any stories of their life together. Nothing. She kept Father locked inside her just as she kept everything else locked inside of her. It had been the same when Grandfather died, when she had told me nothing about how she felt, how she had loved her father, if it hurt her not having him around, if she missed him. Knowing how she was, I asked her nothing. Her life remained as unchangeable as ever.

I, on the other hand, found an escape from my countless losses in the innumerable responsibilities of Nothing. Without Father to guide and support me, I was faced with managing that vast estate and the productive variety of its circular and perpetual calendars. On all accounts, I truly became Luísa from Nothing.

The time of my generation had arrived. Nothing had been handed over to me by fate, and I was the heir of the generation that was dying on me. As all generations that arrive in their time, I wanted to claim my dignity and impart the signature that legitimised me as the head of Nothing.

I bought a Ford 2N, a robust tractor designed during war, and time in Nothing started to run faster. I taught our manager's son to drive that heavy, panzer-like piece of machinery and sent him for a while to a garage in Alhandra where he could learn some mechanics. I was filled with the wish of modernising Nothing. Father had had electricity brought in, and I was going to dedicate myself to the new technologies that increased productivity or that allowed tasks to be performed more swiftly.

The work and the new ideas blunted the raw pain of mourning and helped staunch the bile I spat at Mother. I owe it to Nothing for having sustained and calmed me in that hour of death.

Every once in a while, Father's request that I try to understand Mother and love her resurfaced to remind me of my promise to look after her without any resentments. Little by little, I began to allay my anger. I determined I should trust the words Father had given me. After all, he knew Mother better than I did. The problem was, I had no idea how to communicate with her. And it felt painful and artificial to be near her.

Slowly I summoned the strength that could give me the courage to start a path that might lead me to her. It had to be and, if for no other reason, at least out of obligation I would have to muster the will to approach her.

On a warm afternoon in the spring following Father's death, I asked Engrácia to set a table under the loquat tree in the backyard garden where the peacocks used to roam and where, many years before, I used to sit writing my diaries about days full of the life ahead of me, the whole waiting to be written. I chose a tablecloth of green and white plaid, picked a yellow rose with a dark pink trim all around the petals which I put in a tall cut-glass vase, and made tea. Then I invited Mother to join me.

When she came down and out the door leading to the garden, I was already sitting at the table, waiting for her. Through the lenses of the sunglasses Antero had given me, I saw she had combed her hair a little bit, as if to go out, and had put on a light cardigan, the pale blue of which matched her icy eyes. From the soft look on her face, I realised she had appreciated the invitation. I was glad of that. We had tea without engaging in much conversation, preferring instead to enjoy the glorious afternoon.

That day I started to feel her presence. That woman was my only family and, more than anything else, she was my mother. That had to be a more than enough reason for me, and somehow I would have to be able to find some sort of warm feeling for her. I gave myself and us the chance for discovery. The old hatchet could finally be buried.

Henceforth, I started to protect the occasional afternoon, borrowed from my unending chores, to have tea with her. Not that we talked much but, in time, I discovered that those silent pauses were not as uncomfortable as they had once been. Even in silence, I learned, we communicated in the language of the presence of one another. Maybe Father had known that language and, for that matter, understood her better than I did. Yes, I learned that we do not need the oral sound of words to communicate. I started to be filled with a respect for Mother I had hitherto thought impossible. It was not doting love, it was some other feeling. A different emotion allowed by the infinite multiplicity with which feelings are made.

One day I decided to go to Mother's sitting-room and ask her to join me for a walk in the lush vineyards covered in new, verdant leaves. It was sunny and nice. The fields were decorated in the luxurious green of vines sprouting with life and another year of grapes.

Unannounced and swiftly, I entered the room. And interrupted something. Some event was abruptly cut short, but I knew not what it was. I felt as if someone had hidden quickly behind the drapes which were swaying gently, as though a light breeze or person had brushed them. I had intruded on something, but there was nothing there. On Mother's lap lay a book with colourful images and children's stories.

Taken by the surprise provoked by the interruption I myself had caused, I barely uttered what had taken me there. A strange familiarity with an interrupted scene many years before was eerily creeping down my spine as indefinite memories I could not put into words were awakened in my mind. In sharp contrast to Mother's staggering calm, I felt intrusive and flummoxed. The image of my son sitting on her lap, on the day he vanished and I found him in her chambers, quietly flipping through a book, was sending shock waves all over me.

Amidst excuses and half muttered words, I left the room. I was disturbed by what I had seen without seeing. Could it be that António was on his Grandmother's lap browsing through books of tales? How silly of me! My mind was playing tricks, and memories of my son were resurfacing from out of nowhere. I imputed my hallucination to my mad attempts at denying how much I missed my son by overburdening myself with the labours of Nothing. Guilt lambasted me. My heart as a mother, my anguished, bleeding heart, was throwing me into this moment of insanity because, in the midst of my many chores, I was neglecting his memory, failing to think of António as often as I owed him and the heart of my maternity.

Rationalising the incident, I locked it away in my mind, thinking it a result of loss-after-loss induced folly.

That night, nonetheless, I asked Engrácia to tell me what she knew about Mother's visions.

"O, My Child, why do you ask me such things? Those were things the people said. Forget about them."

But I knew there were things in a past before me. I went back to being the little girl in braids who grilled Engrácia about stories of werewolves and who not would be put off by the negatives and detours she could find to thwart my nosy curiosity.

"Yes, Child, there was talk of things," was Engrácia's vexed answer when I insisted on the question.

"But what things, Engrácia?"

I kept on asking, because I wanted light to be shed on Mother's past and on what I thought I had seen earlier in her room.

"Foolish things. I don't remember."

"Of course you do," I insisted. "You just don't want to tell me. Come on, tell me!"

"I don't know. People said she played with two children no one ever saw."

"What children?"

"Children. A boy and a little girl. Blond, I guess. I don't know. You know how children are. They invent things."

"Indeed, but in Mother's case it was more than child's imagination, wasn't it?"

Engrácia would say no more, going silent in that awkwardness that is characteristic of knowing more and not wanting to disclose things she did not wish resurrected. Things which were so ancient she could hardly attribute either to truth or fabulation. Things fragmented by the passing of time and memory.

"And it wasn't only children, was it?" I went on. "I know about the seamstress. Father said Mother would hear her sewing in the corner of the sitting-room. But that must be some electrical phenomenon going through those walls. Maybe a piece of iron that was left there and attracts electric currents. It is the visions I want you to tell me about."

"I don't know Child. It's been so long. Why all these questions now?"

"Curiosity, Engrácia. Curiosity...."

But with her question, Engrácia shut me up. In no way was I going to reveal why suddenly it had crossed my mind to ask her about strange things from a distant past. I had no inclination to let her know that, in a moment overcome with inexplicable madness, I thought I had caught Mother playing with someone in her study. It was ridiculous, that. I put a stop to the conversation and decided to definitely close my mind to the incident. After all, I was the one who had created ghosts by having my son's room walled.

Setting those thoughts aside, I turned on the radio for a diversion.

From the news, it was possible to detect a shift in the war. The Allies had landed on the shores of Normandy and were claiming victory upon victory on the European front. We did not yet know about the horrors waiting to be found or the bombs that would put an end to the conflict, but I was confident we would emerge with peace and could hardly wait for the day when there was no more want and no more rationing, no more battles and no more death.

I longed for the end of the war and for the passing of time that would take me further and further from Father's death and my repeated losses. I longed for the end of the war as a bird longs to fly in infinite skies.

I wished for some new chapter to take me away from a stubbornly present past.

XXI

I have no fond memories of the 1940s or my thirties. Back then, I used to wish hard for time to fly. The war, the rationing, the droughts, the devastating hurricane, all the deaths. I wished to die before having to bury Mother. Life had no meaning to me. I forgot I was already dead.

I was saved by Nothing. The ever Nothing.

I began mechanizing the farm and ordered books to instruct myself in agricultural sciences. Possessed of this new knowledge I experimented with electric brooders and new chemicals for the treatment of vine diseases. I modernised the cellar and created a brand: *Nothing's*. I had elegant labels made for the dark green bottles in which our wine was sold.

Known as Luísa from Nothing, I now became the Mistress of Nothing. The mistress implying some sort of title that marked both my possession of Nothing and my being possessed by it. The lover and the commander, the owner and the slave. To the eternal dichotomy of my name as Luísa and Matilde, this new dichotomy was added to characterise my relationship with Nothing: Luísa from Nothing and the Mistress of Nothing. Daughter of Nothing. Owner of Nothing. Luísa from Nothing, a name in full. Neither the daughter nor the wife of someone. I was the person, that person. In those patriarchal times I was something of a freak. Without a husband, male siblings or a father, I belonged entirely to myself. Maybe it was because of that people started calling me the Mistress of Nothing. Only Nothing possessed me as a spouse. And, in turn, it was to Nothing that I gave myself in the whole of my body and my soul.

In 1951, I turned forty and found great relief in it. True, I felt a chronic aching now that I knew I would never bear living children again. I would never again feel them growing in my womb or hold a little hand in mine or smell the smell of a baby of mine. The relief I felt was the lightness found in the certainty of not having to go through more losses. If I conceived no more, I would lose no more.

The matter was thus settled. Also, the relentlessness of age solved, once and for all, the pressing question of my contributing to the succession of Nothing. If nothing could be done, then case closed. Full stop.

Because Father had died, I had already been through that loss. That pain I had suffered, so it was no longer in my path. I had waged that battle and I could now have a truce. It was as if a compulsory and unpleasant chapter was ended. Obviously, dealing with loss is a daily, unending affair, but the actual process of Father's death was dead and done. If I had already mourned him, I would no longer live in the fear of losing him. That atrocious pain was behind me. The moment of having him taken from me was past. I could, and would, still weep; however I would not be crying on account of the amputation of a recent now. These were the tears of having loved, the tears of missing a beloved presence. But that hurt grew tamer, more familiar, friendly even, and faithful.

Likewise, dispossessed of both living and unborn children, I would not have to be afraid of losing them, just as I would never lose them.

Mother was showing no signs of aging, but I knew I would not feel her death in the same violent way I had lived Father's death — with all that desperate hoping before coming to the acceptance of the final end. I had Engrácia. I understood her mortality as a natural occurrence in someone who was bound by nature to depart ahead of me. And, frankly, I was truly convinced she would not leave us anytime soon.

Indeed, it was with utmost relief that I welcomed my forties and, in addition, the new decade. Loss, I believed, was far from my horizon, and that soothed my grief-laden soul.

I started going to the movies in Vila Franca on days when there were matinées. Once or twice I even invited Mother. Her spirit, however, had no wish for the intrusion of sounds and images of others on the words she read in the silence of her mind. It made absolute sense to me that she did not want to tarnish her books with the technicolour images of cinema. I was not in the least surprised. After all, she was true to herself. As she had not appreciated the radio when Father introduced it to our house, how could she possibly welcome the combined mix of sound and image together?

One day I took Engrácia to watch a movie featuring Groucho Marx, Frank Sinatra and Jane Russell. It was called *Double Dynamite*, and Engrácia spent days and days telling everyone how that cinema thing was "so beautiful, oh, so beautiful."

Portuguese cinema had by then stagnated compared to the previous decade, when it had experienced a boom and popularity that were never to come again. Gone were the comedies with the great Vasco Santana and António Silva. But I had been struggling with so many things back then that time and patience failed me, and the big screen had passed me by altogether. Besides, our rural Nothing was a world away from such innovations.

On the surface, everything seemed to be well. But my shell remained hollow. I was still dead. Had I stopped to think, maybe I would not have wanted to live. I refrained from those thoughts, though. I had to. Too much depended on me to afford thinking about myself or my selfish choices, which, who knows, might have granted me some simulation of a life.

I did not see you for a long time. It was almost as if in having given you Father, you had been satiated. Had you not made a momentary appearance when Jacinto got trapped under the tractor, I would almost have forgotten about you.

Once in a while there were accidents on the farm: normal things occurring from the handling of dangerous tools and implements with sharp edges and blades. Not normal was Jacinto's dying under the capsized tractor that fell over the ravine I had so often told him to avoid. It was the worst of accidents.

He left two young children, and I took them under my wing. At night they would sleep in the house of our manager, their grandfather, but I was the one who sent them to school and who was waiting for them at tea time and helped them study and supervised the homework they did on the big table of our kitchen. I was not trying to fill the unfillable void of my children. Neither was I moved by any instincts of a surrogate motherhood.

The vision of children or being near them was still a painful thing. The slightest touch or memory could reopen my scars, leaving me bleeding and aching. No, I was interested in the well-being of those two children because of the gratitude I owed their father for everything he had done for Nothing. Looking at them I pitied their fate as one who succumbs to abandoned milky-eyed puppies begging for love. Thus they lived under my protection while life carried on in Nothing.

A bloody industrialist, full of himself, came over one day. He owned a small factory of animal feed near Sacavém, or in the vicinity of that Lisboan periphery, which was totally alien to me and that I, not knowing it in the least, was absolutely convinced I hated. He was fecund with ownership and a domineering attitude. For a split second I was reminded of the Marquis of Cabreza, but unlike him, this gentleman was not here because of me.

"How much do you want for all of this?" he asked, raising his arm to draw a circle in the air that indicated the whole of Nothing. He wanted to buy the farm from me.

"It's not for sale."

"Make a price and I'll buy it."

"I told you, it's not for sale."

"C'me on! Everything is for sale," he insisted, with that arrogance that does not take no for an answer.

"Well, Nothing isn't, and shan't be, for sale. I appreciate your interest but today we won't make a deal," I retorted, hiding the fact that I had no patience for that kind of talk.

I said goodbye in the politeness of a "good afternoon," and he drove off in the Mercedes of success along with his frustrated intents.

After that I had to give a strip of land to the municipality so they could build a road connecting Ladeirinhas to Casal do Mirão, a tiny hamlet in that vicinity. All of a sudden, or so it seemed, everyone had discovered Nothing, and Nothing interested everyone.

The macadam road was inaugurated. In our country, so infinitely far from the city, the road now open was traversed by pack donkeys and carts pulled by mules, and I considered it much having been done about nothing. All the bother and the fuss to open a road that served the same purposes as the age-old trails and paths that had always been so useful to our rural way of life. Macadam itself was not to my liking. The white, fine dust that covered everything and suffocated the lone pedestrian each time a rare motor vehicle passed by was beyond irritating. So, I had blackthorn shrubs planted on the side of the road to hold the dust.

Little by little, we were moving forward in history and becoming part of a world going by the name of *Modern*.

As usual with the owners of Nothing in office, I embraced the role of benefactor of Ladeirinhas. I paid for the church roof repairs and had new vestments bought for the priest. I was not moved by faith or the belief in a God I treated with indifference. I accepted the bills as an encumbrance, a service that was expected from someone like me. The priest invited me to oversee the progress of the repairs and, resigned to what had to be had to be, I endured the visits and all his explanations about the many needs of the parish and how my charity was a grace I rendered the Almighty. Of course that was neither I fooling him nor would he let himself be fooled. We addressed one another courteously and played the part. When the round was over, I sighed with relief.

I bought shoes for the schoolchildren of Ladeirinhas. A law had come out making it compulsory to wear shoes to school. But not everyone had the money to buy their children shoes, so these were passed on from siblings to cousins and back to siblings. I had a truckload of shoes sent to the school so all kids could have a pair. Later I found out they carried the shoes tied by the shoelaces and hanging around their necks. They would rather go barefoot than imprison their calloused feet, toughened by walking on dirt and gravel, squeezed into new shoes. I laughed at the money misspent and the intelligent stubbornness with which the children detoured the imposition. The ingenuity and creativity of tender age made me smile.

Bit by bit, the ancient world of Nothing was flowing through the hourglass and disappearing. It was not an overnight disappearance but, rather like the sluggish flow of thick honey, it steadily seeped away. The more that was lost, the more I found myself in charge of a

Nothing that was less and less like the Nothing in which I had grown up with Grandfather and Father: The Nothing of oxen-ploughed fields, of werewolves and *gaibéus*, who, like clockwork, always arrived at the time of olives. Even the clarity of the days we lived seemed different from the endless blue light of the past we always tend to embellish.

Then in 1955 I lost Engrácia. Her larger-than-life energy had begun to wane, and she had adopted the old woman's habit of wearing a scarf tied around her head. She said the slightest breeze gave her migraines so violent her eyes popped out. She complained about rheumatism. And her fingers made crooked by much use and the bitter winters they had endured helped me see her life as a string of many long years.

As I had done with Father, I took her to Doctor D'Além, who could do nothing more than prescribe for her a liniment to soothe her aching bones and cod liver oil to strengthen her. When he finished his consultation with her, he called me aside and, in the fatherly wisdom of someone who knows what is about to unfold, told me:

"Resign yourself to the facts, *Dona* Luísa. It's nothing but old age."

Most obviously, I had no intention of resigning to whatever "facts". That would mean going against my nature of impulses and moving forward. Nevertheless, if there was one thing Father's death and all the Calvary leading to it had taught me, it was that I should tone down my rush to get into the fight of lost battles.

Since I was a middle woman, here I was, up for the part once more, and play it masterly I would.

Aware of Engrácia's tendency to believe the unbelievable, that included my Mother's ghosts, werewolves and Saint Barbara, I had a witchdoctor brought over from Valflores. Her verdict on the condition could not have been any more appropriate: the evil eye.

Over a basin filled with water, into which she had added a drop of olive oil, the witchdoctor held her hand and recited Saint Cyprian's prayer to exorcise the affliction, as Engrácia stood by.

"As a servant of God and His creature, evil spirit loose from what it has bound…"

I paid her five thousand *réis*[39] – somehow I never got used to saying escudos–and rested my soul, knowing I was giving Engrácia the comfort of her convictions and of that past where she had lived most of her life that was now fading away.

Engrácia had raised me. In my feverish nights of colds and being ill, she had tucked me in to sleep; she had bathed me and braided my hair to go to classes; she had sewn the skirts and blouses I wore, had taught me to be a woman and explained life to me. More than my own Mother, Engrácia was the closest thing I had to a mother.

I tried to delay your coming.

Religiously, I would myself go to the chemist's to fetch the medicines which were nothing more than placebos to cure what could not be cured.

Anticipating you, I bought a plot in the cemetery at Ladeirinhas so she could stay next to us as she had always been. With time on my hands, I took care of everything. Therefore, when she died, you were already expecting her and I could hand her over to you quietly and in peace.

I had become experienced in these matters and knew exactly what I had to do in these moments of mediation.

Engrácia had died and taken with her another piece of the Nothing that was running out and away from this time. My role was ending, and Mother was all there was left. I was relieved by the knowledge that my labours were almost finished.

---

39. *Réis*, plural of real, the Portuguese currency prior to the introduction of the escudo in 1911, which, in turn, was replaced by the euro in 1999. One thousand *réis* corresponded to one escudo.

40. Émile Zola (1840-1902), the French novelist whose work is renowned as the precursor of Naturalism in literature, with themes of human life being conditioned by external facts and literature emulating real life. His *Les Mystères de Marseille* (1867) was translated into English and published as *The Mysteries of Marseilles* in 1895.

Eça de Queirós (1845-1900), a Portuguese novelist considered the most representative author of realist aesthetic in Portuguese literature. Heavily influenced by, and like Zola, Queirós believed literature should reflect real life. Translated into many languages, his most notable novels include *O Crime do Padre Amaro [The Sin of Father Amaro]* (1875) and *Os Maias [The Maias]* (1888), still widely read and frequently adapted to television and cinema.

Marcel Proust (1871-1922), the French novelist best known for his work *À la recherche du temps perdu*, a novel in seven volumes published between 1913 and 1927, and translated into English as *In Search of Lost Time*.

Machado de Assis (1839-1908), a Brazilian novelist, playwright and essayist, is considered to have introduced Realism in Brazilian literature with his novel *Memórias Póstumas de Brás Cubas* (1881), also translated into English as *Posthumous Memoirs of Bras Cubas*, sometimes carrying the subtitle, *the Epitaph of a Small Winner*. Assis maintained a long-lasting literary feud with the Portuguese Eça de Queirós by saying that, on giving emphasis to reality, Queirós had neglected the aesthetic beauty of literature.

XXII

Life is a winding road of ironies. Much as we wish to control it, we cannot, and naïve we are to think we can at the times we think we can. For we always think we can.

I was also like that: I thought I could control life. Had I managed it, though, I would not have ended up losing everyone and being left alone with Mother, precisely the being with whom I had found it most difficult to relate during that life I so tried to domesticate and bring under my will.

It took me years to get used to the idea that it was with Mother, and Mother alone, that I was to spend my days at Nothing. With Engrácia gone, the house entered the silence of Mother. I missed Engrácia's chattering and her constant scolding the maids she said never made anything right and were always thinking about boys. Without Engrácia around, I had no one waiting for me at the end of the day after I had checked on Mother to greet her and see whether she was alright and ask her about her day. We spoke little, Mother and I. My forced training to get accustomed to her had borne some fruits, but I would not go as far as saying we ever got any closer than the cordiality stemming from habit or routine.

I learned she enjoyed Zola and Eça de Queirós, had read Proust and Machado de *Assis*.[40] I found out she could elaborate with great breadth and depth on theological and philosophical matters. She did so sparingly, and that added to the enigmatic aura I had always seen in her. One day I asked her straightforwardly:

"Do you still hear the seamstress?"

"Yes," she said, and nodded, the tone of her voice giving away no sort of discomfort, either at the question or the so unconventional answer as the explanation for the phenomenon that my ears had never actually heard but my rational mind attributed to some explicable electric energy going through the wall.

"And does anyone know who she is?"

"Does that matter?"

"Plain curiosity, Mother. I thought you might know who that lady was when she was alive or why she is forced to sew in the Hereafter."

"I never asked her."

Silence struck me like a blow. The answer confirmed that Mother talked to the ghost seamstress inhabiting our house. Had I not known Mother, I would be inclined to think the madness of old age and crazy Argentina's genes were getting to her as she advanced into her years.

Baffled and stranded halfway between fear and the curiosity of asking her more, time was suspended for me in the prolonged, swift instant it took me to decide to carry on the conversation.

"She comes here often, then?"

"Not always. Sometimes she goes to other houses."

"And do other people come here?" I asked, remembering my suspicions about the presence I had sensed several years before.

"Sometimes." The answer came with her usual impassiveness. She raised a gold-edged cup to her lips and I knew, as I always knew, that the conversation was over. Mother reentered her world. It was as though she had only come to visit us for a while, and it was now time to go back.

I resumed sipping the Darjeeling tea I had brought for us on that greyish afternoon of dawning autumn. We kept still until I got up and took back the tray with the fine English china cups and saucers of the trousseau made for her when she got married in 1909.

I could not help but think about how natural and easy it was for Mother to talk about those things and agreed that the life of semi-seclusion she led was the only possible one in a world so alien to her. I accepted the ghosts and did not fear their being real. After all, they had been with me forever, and I had no need to see or hear them for them to exist. There were certain realities in life that called for no rational understanding, and Mother made me realise that, keenly. Maybe Mother's world was simpler than ours. Needing less verbalisation and conferring no oddity to what we, in this world, find different, perhaps it was a world where existence was smoother and more undisturbed.

By degrees, driven by the companionship life forced us to share, I began to see Mother as a representative of that other, parallel world.

Even if she were not, at least I believed so and that believing mitigated the questions and doubts I knew would be left unanswered. In consequence, I could free my spirit from the eternal question: Why, why did she have to be like that?

Not questioning, I learnt, can bring tremendous peace to a mind constantly beset with riddles.

On another afternoon of tea served in ancient porcelain and whitish horizons of light mist, she told me, midst her distinctive vague gaze, she would like me to use her study when she died.

"It's cool in the summer and bathed by morning sun. It will make a fine office."

Allowing myself to enjoy a long sip of that dark, crimson-gold tea, I accepted the offer. It was, all at once, a sort of incumbency, a legacy, and an eloquent gesture among all Mother's singular gestures.

"Yes, Mother. But that's still very far away."

We resumed the shared silence which of usual ended our conversation but not the company of one another. And I let my eyes take in the space she had just given me, adding that immense rest to the shelf in the bookcase where she had been keeping my diaries for so long. Composing the total amount of the room I was now inheriting.

It would also be amongst silences flavoured with tea in the strange and simultaneously familiar companionship we had with each other that I was to understand the essence of my Uncle Romano. After a life of curiosity as to why people said he was a wild ass, out of Mother's staring at the distance and a dialogue of unpronounceable words and guessed ideas finally came the certainty that was hers entirely.

"So that was a protection?" I asked, the day I embarked on the subject of Uncle being an ass. The non-word which came as a reply settled all the suspicion forming in my mind. Uncle liked men in a time of castrating orthodoxies. The asses giving off sparks from under their hooves and running unbridled in the dark of night across deserted roads and lone crossings were social pariahs. Out of disgust and misunderstanding, the people would rather know them as werewolves, aberrant creatures in their anti-natural ways, than men.

Aberration was a valid explanation for the deviant behaviour and that justification served as protection: No one went after werewolves. There were unhallowed nights of full moon when a man might become a wild animal — a red-eyed wolf or wild mule or donkey, as folklore would have people believe — and on those nights no one ventured out for fear of encountering such cursed, unnatural creatures. The people were happy assuming these were men atoning for some sin rather than think the truth that they were men-loving men who gathered under cover of the night and myth. Nobody messed with werewolves and werewolves messed with no one, and it was all very fine. Better to leave some things alone. Facing homosexuality would have been far more complicated than coming across werewolves, men transformed into hideous asses. Werewolves could be explained; men who liked men could not.

Mother had lived all her life knowing who Uncle Romano truly was. I am ignorant of whether Father was aware of who or what his brother was, even as I am in the dark as to whether Mother ever told him the truth about Uncle. In any case, the certainty I had just found out made me look at her in a new light, among the many in which I was now starting to see her. I admired her tolerant acceptance. Perhaps the many books she read had acquainted her with the normality of other possibilities of life. Or maybe she was just like that. In her difference from us and the rest of the world, herself a being inhabiting a limbo, so, too, she might understand and accept the werewolves as kindred souls. I do not know. I do know that in those times of rigour and the tight corset of morals, she had seen nothing weird about Uncle Romano. She had not questioned. She had not been surprised.

At the end of that conversation I could not help looking with new awareness at Mother's gaze. That staring at far-off and invisible horizons was not seeing things from here. Her eyes of blue water saw instead the world in which she resided, a world of other dimensions, of topographies neither geographic nor finite. I joined the silent conversation into which Mother had let us enter and, with her, joined my gaze to the horizon beyond Nothing.

Unaware as to why, that proximity and that mute sharing with her warmed my heart. In that diffuse instant, rendered almost ethereal by our staring into the distance, I felt happy for having a mother. Most of all, I felt suffused by a faint warmth for my mother being that woman there. I was never going to hug her. Never was I going to lose myself as a daughter in the warmth of her embrace as I had with Father. Never ever would I tell her I loved her. Any displays of affection between us would be lost for all eternity. My heart was aware of that loss but shielded itself by being shut and accepting of the unchangeable distancing with which that woman treated her human relationships.

Throughout my life I had been the recipient of my Mother's strange love; a love characterised by a paucity of forms and words but always one of tremendous impact. With only a few actions she had told me a thousand things in my lifetime. The letter she had written to me during my mourning in Ericeira, the shelf she had offered me in her precious bookcase, the name she had told me to give my son. In the rare moments she had made an appearance in my life, albeit her everlasting presence, she had always had a profound effect on my heart and my memory. Moreover, in her peculiar way of being, she had also taught me. From her, I learned that we are but a mere passage. I had tied Father to an artificial life whereas all she wanted was to free him. I had deemed her cold when she was far too wise of the vain things of this life, knowing, thereof, we should not cling to the meaninglessness of trying to change that which cannot be changed.

Strangely, gradually, I started to grow accustomed to my Mother. In the utter loneliness of people my life had become after so many deaths, and my own, I got closer to her and thus loosed myself from my orphanhood of her.

I got used to those rituals. Mistress of Nothing, not always was I aware of the passing of time. It is so when the soul inhabits a place beyond mortality, for life is of little interest. A place without children growing, without love blossoming. My time was a petty thing of seasons of sowing and harvesting, of rains and suns, that circular, non-continuous time. That was my time.

"There's a gentleman in the living-room waiting for you."

"A gentleman?"

I was coming from the vegetable garden with a bundle of radishes, my apron soiled with the mud of having plucked them out of the wet soil, when the maid came to the kitchen with the message. I laid the radishes on the thick, pink marble counter, undid the knot of the apron and thought it must be another nosy, bossy someone wanting to buy Nothing.

"But who the hell is the gentleman? Did he, at least, say his business here?"

Questioning the girl was to no avail. How I missed Engrácia and her solicitous ways of receiving visitors, her ability to give straightforward messages, the way she made my life so much easier.

"He said you know who he is and that he wishes to have a quick word with you. His name is Arturo."

"Arturo? I don't know any Arturo!"

Completely lost for any Arturos that might come knocking at my door, I hastened to the living-room, determined to have him know Nothing was not for sale. Giving a quick fix to my undone hair in order to make myself more presentable for what he was about to hear, self-confident and swift I walked the wood floor of the corridor tred by the many years of Nothing.

I came to a halt, stalled by the sight beyond the door.

XXIII

"You look the same, Luísa."

The calm voice was familiar. The voice of a bygone, remote past.

In a fraction of the millisecond of the longest perplexity ever to have struck me, I thought how Engrácia was right in saying those girls working at our house were a lost case. Antero was standing in my living-room, the living-room of Nothing, right in front of me. The Antero of a time before. Antero. I caught my reflection in his eyes so similar to mine when he took off his sunglasses: sunglasses exactly like those he had given me and that I always had with me for protection against excessive glare.

Antero, right there before me. He was still lean and tall, just as I remembered him. His hair had started to gray at the temples, and he retained the same air of serene sadness I recalled from meeting him in Ericeira, in what now seemed centuries before.

"Antero..." I whispered, even as an overwhelming clairvoyance, allowed by the instinct of certainty, told me I was going to bury him.

I felt my knees giving way, such was the seismic wave sweeping over my body.

"Please," I invited him, with a gesture indicating a green leather couch with brass studs where he could sit. Still flummoxed and short for words, I did not know how to say the simplest, "Sit down, please," so I relied on the neutrality of gestures and half-words.

"Forgive me, Luísa, for invading your space unannounced, for barging in like this. I myself had no idea if I was coming."

I let him speak because, frankly, I did not know what to say. There was nothing I wanted to say, and my silent surprise was wordier than any my mouth could have uttered. Not speaking calmed me and forced me to listen to what I already knew without knowing.

"I've never stopped thinking about you," he continued after realising I was not going to interrupt him. "I moved on with my life, but you were always there in a place I couldn't hide from myself. It has taken me these last two years to make up my mind to come here, and I don't know what lies ahead. I only know I had to come. I'm free, as you might guess."

I nodded, the affirmation telling him I understood he had come because his wife had died. "In short," he continued, "I expect nothing. I know nothing of your life, of you, of your heart. I came because I had to come. I had to see you and tell you that whatever you wish will be; whatever you tell me, shall be." I stared at him for a long while, looking at the future and contemplating the present into which our past had materialised. The past I had been losing, painful bit after painful bit, had come to me.

"You're a good man, Antero," I said, my eyes fixed on him for the eternity of that moment. The sentence had come out of me without my realising I was going to say anything. Indeed, I hoped words could be swifter than my thoughts, confused by a thousand visions and memories. I trusted the sound of words, because I could not trust my entangled thoughts. "I'm glad you came. I never imagined you would".

"I know," he interjected, as if to affirm that he fully realised the extent of my bewilderment.

"I never thought of anything after all that. I didn't even have the chance to thank you for the glasses."

"Neither were you supposed to."

"I know. That's not what I wanted to tell you. A million things are going through my mind, and I don't know where to start or what to say. "

"Say nothing, Luísa. I also don't know what I'd say if a stranger came rushing in through the door saying these things."

"You're not a stranger."

Moving toward him, I knelt in front of him. I wanted to look at him, close up and straight in the eye. I wanted him to know with certainty there was nothing wrong in his surprising attitude. I wanted to let him know I admired his courage.

"You're not a stranger, Antero. You're here now, and that's all I care."

I let him draw near and touch my lips with his. It was the gentle, soft kiss of old lovers reunited once more. Lovers who had been satiated long ago and had no need now for the voraciousness of a first time. Lovers who had found out time is all they have.

The kiss lasted a lifetime and beyond. It lasted the exact amount of time needed to build the bridge from the past on a faraway shore. When it ended, he slid from the polished leather of the couch, kneeling in front of me for a tight embrace, as we prolonged the reunion. As I hugged him, I felt his warmth and the familiarity of a body that would be mine henceforth.

I stood up and gave him my hand, motioning for him to follow me. Once again I understood the value of there being no words because, no matter how grand and eloquent they might be, words could not capture this moment, because not all moments can be captured by words. Moments prevail over words. I was my Mother's daughter.

I guided him through the corridors of the centuries-old house of Nothing. I led him up the heavily handrailed, wood staircase. I opened the door to my bedroom, an inviolate room where no man had ever been.

I was the mistress of Nothing and there was nothing I could not do.

Gently, I took off his jacket. Gently, I unbuttoned his shirt while we looked at each other with the same blue-water eyes we shared, and he unbuttoned my blouse. Slowly, as two who have the time of Time, we gazed at one another with the smiling eyes of rediscovery.

I made love for the first time. It was not the discovery crisscrossed with rationalizations of the first time with António. It was not the uncommitted sex that served to erase the past of the first time with Antero. It was not the wild, unrestrained lust of Ángel. This was something new. And this new thing was love, respect, the wanting to give because I was receiving: the selfless giving of someone who is also receiving. And it was on my bed, in my room. It was loving in the space of my I. And this man loved and respected me. He had carried me in his mind and in his heart like a shackle for years, and the moment was now liberating him. For that reason, all this was a gift.

In slow motion, we explored our bodies with our fingertips, our eyes in no hurry to see ahead. I loved his age in the tiny wrinkles of a skin already starting to sag on his thin neck. Between my breasts, once full of round, there was now a long, vertical line born out of habit. We had changed, although we were the same. More loving because older. More secure, more aware of the time we had. I closed my eyes and allowed myself to be transported to a primordial space which was the Nothing where freedom was I. A space of sun. Pasts, presents and futures. I closed my eyes to be everything where there was no time, no space, no nothing.

When I returned, we were facing one another, and he was stroking the hair that framed my face.

"Marry me."

"No," I answered, with a serene smile. He smiled back, unperturbed, still looking at me in the rapture of the moment.

There was nothing that could destroy the peace for us. Nothing that could break the spell of our getting back together and the love made between the sheets of my bed. I did not care what the maids might be thinking or what the people working in Nothing, and from there to Ladeirinhas, would say. Little did I mind whether Father was watching from Above and worrying about what the people were once more going to say about me. My thoughts were far from Engrácia's sermons about what I did to my life. At the end of the day, I knew there was only one person in the world who would not reprove me: Mother. Mother, who had one day written to tell me my will was what mattered the most. Mother, who had written me precisely when my will dictated I was Antero's lover. Mother, who was now the only link I had brought with me from the past of forever.

In another of life's tremendous ironies, Mother would understand this act of mine and whatever concubinage I chose.

I lingered in the quiet rest afforded by Antero's gazing at me, the companionship of our bodies on that afternoon of nearing autumn and darker greys enveloping the room in the twilight I call sleep. I felt peace.

XXIV

Gradually, Antero moved to Nothing. Of course, it went without saying that if any change was to happen because of our relationship, it had to come from him. I was a tree, its roots deeply embedded in the fertile soil of Nothing. I was a mighty oak that no storm could topple. I was Nothing and Nothing was I.

My afternoon teas with Mother went on, and I did not need abundant words to tell her I intended to live in the company of this man. I introduced them one day over dinner after inviting her to join us downstairs. They were polite to one another, and I could sense they established a tacit pact of non-interference in their respective spaces. Antero was a man of peace and, hurt by life just as I had been, would never call forth unnecessary hostilities. And Mother, well, Mother was Mother and since nothing upset her, everything would be alright. Besides, I knew she understood, and so there was no hurdle there.

"Your house in Ericeira. I bought it," he informed me one day when we were having lunch *al fresco* under the dense shade of the loquat tree.

"The house . . ." I exhaled the words as the memory they evoked rushed in.

"I bought it soon after the time of us. I needed things that made me feel you."

I looked at him as I always looked at him, in admiration mixed with a rich feeling which I imagine is what people call love. I loved Antero, not with the untamed, intense love with which I had loved my children and not with the silk-like love I felt for Father. This was much different. I loved Antero out of mutual delight. We enjoyed each other's company. We took pleasure in sharing silences full of words. He liked keeping me company when I went riding in my rounds of Nothing, and that also made me love him more. Few things in life have given me so much pleasure as showing him all of Nothing and its recesses, telling him its stories and how Nothing came to be.

One day I took him to the vault. I opened its green, cast iron doors and glass window panes and introduced him to my dead. Looking him in the eye, I used my thoughts to silently invite him to find his repose there, to know I would like that.

He understood, and I saw him smile in agreement. Antero would join the Boshoff from Nothing.

"Marry me," he asked once more, taken by the solemn intimacy of meeting my kin and being invited to be one of us for all eternity.

I nodded in acceptance, with one condition.

"Only in a civil ceremony."

"It shall be so."

We got married at the Civil Registry Conservatory in Vila Franca. In 1958, a wedding without a religious ceremony was not a frequent occurrence. It was almost a half-marriage, but I did not mind. I did not take his name, and we married under full separation of patrimony.[41] It seems I had, after all, imposed a lot of conditions to assent to something I regarded as a prison, although I had once, back in my faraway youth, prepared to marry with all the pomp and all the circumstance.

Antero brought no children from his marriage to the sickly, frail woman who had left him in widowerhood. I was not insensitive to that fact. Among all the reasons and more I had despised the advances of the Marquis of Cabreza, the children he would bring as an attachment to remind me of my own had been the greatest obstacle. Antero's lack of children was healing to my soul, as we both knew what it was to live without the love of children. That similarity united us, and it was why I had agreed to marry him. On the other hand, because we had climbed steep paths in our separate lives, we could maintain our respective individualities: neither of us trying to negate or pressure the other.

---

41. Patrimony is a literal translation of the Portuguese, "património," which refers to the estates of a spouse or couple. By law, marriage can be with separation of the respective estates or, as was usual in the old days, the estates of both spouses united after the wedding. In this case, Luísa opted to have a separation of all her possessions from her husband's: finances, estate, and full inheritance.

I had arrived as Luísa from Nothing through a long, winding Calvary and was not disposed to let Matilde, whoever she was now signing those papers, alter that identity. For again, I was made aware that it was Matilde taking over the social and documentary stage of my life. Matilde was in the certificates of my baptism and communion. Matilde lived in the birth and death certificates of my children. Matilde signed for this marriage. She shone in the solemnities of my life, and I had to bear life. However, Matilde's days were numbered. One day, when the papers turned into dust, she would be no more. And on the day Mother died, the very sound of her name would be silenced. I was Luísa, and the married Matilde would be left unaccompanied in some drawer at the Civil Conservatory.

The registrar of the Notary served as our witness, as did Doctor D'Além, of whom I asked the favour. The cold gold of the ring touched the warm skin of my left ring finger and, for the slightest of instants, the shadow of the wing of uncertainty flew over me. Notwithstanding, looking at Antero and seeing the genuine joy only afforded by dreams come true made me cast away sombre feelings and contemplate the step I was taking with optimism. Doctor D'Além congratulated me, saying Daddy would have been very happy.

After the mandatory signatures and greetings, my husband and I made our way back to Nothing, which was no longer my home but, rather, our home.

For a while I nurtured a last hope for a possible pregnancy. My body, however, did not want it. My bedazzlement would have wanted a child, but rationally I was afraid of more losses, and it was more than enough just to have added Antero to my extensive list.

Because, yes, if there was one thing I knew with the certainty of absoluteness, it was that I would have to hand over Antero to you.

Naïvely, I had thought Mother was all that was left to finish my role as a middle woman, but a new variable had entered my life. Now there was this man who would say goodbye to the here with me standing by. Antero was a new obligation I had to make me want to live after him.

It was a paradox: Antero was the only person I voluntarily called into my life of losses and, as such, I charged you nothing for having to give him over to you one day.

We spent our honeymoon at the house in Ericeira, through whose gates I now entered as owner and legitimate wife. We occupied the bedroom that had been mine during the distant autumn when we met and that, during the holidays of his marriage, he had never used out of compunction. We stayed in bed late in the mornings, and in the afternoons we would go to Cabo da Roca, Sintra or Mafra.

I was scared of being happy, knowing that happiness is not a state but a moment.

More often than not, I had to shoo you out of my thoughts and calm down the anxieties of my traumatised heart that was so full of scars. It could not be this hour, now, because now the hour had to be mine.

When we returned to Nothing, the sea sun in our tanned skins, we purchased a television set, another aspect of modernity invading my time and severing connections with my pasts. However, neither he nor I developed an affection for that contraption with its dull grey, serious faces and very proper people in suits and ties. As time passed, the television set became just another dust-covered trinket, and we bought a low cabinet with a double door where we hid it from our sight.

At night, we would sleep wrapped in a tight embrace which held us on to us, and I enjoyed feeling snugged in his arms. That sharing and the velvety softness of skin I felt close to my every inch was the closest I had ever been to heaven. I would fall asleep letting myself slip into the comfortable slumber only possible as two.

Definitely, the 1950s and my forties were lived more light-heartedly than any previous times of my life. In the blue waves of the placid summers at the Ericeira of my marriage, I enjoyed many glimpses of a quieter life. Moreover, I had a husband whose profound soul soothed mine and who knew better than to meddle with my pains, for the sake of leaving them alone and me alone with them. I was entitled to those pains. They were mine, exclusively, not subject to being shared with any marriage.

XXV

The new decade dawned in a new war. This time it was not a war of others. It was a war in our own backyard and, although far in the distant tropics, it was our blood being shed for us. For our generations, it was the third great war our collective fate had thrown into our path. All the male youths from Nothing, and Ladeirinhas, and everywhere else were drafted. Our manager, the father of the late Jacinto, the young tractor man, still had a son at home young enough to join the army. The son went to Santa Margarida for military training and then embarked to Guinea. The hemorrhage of boys was copious.

Flirts between war-godmothers[42] and soldiers sprang out of the air grams the Government implemented as a way to connect the metropolis to the military fighting in the darkest bushes of Africa. Needed trifles to keep spirits up, a palliative to the war effort. Called the National Feminine Movement, the enterprise had been created as an "Association with a legal personality, apolitical and independent from the State, aimed at congregating all Portuguese women interested in paying moral and material support to those fighting for the integrity of the Territory of the Motherland," or so read the Movement's mission statement created by *Dona* Cecília Supico Pinto, the wife of one of Salazar's former ministers.

In spite of not joining the Movement directly, I used the air grams to send comforting words to my godchildren, who were war-godchildren

---

42. In Portugal godparents are both the people who baptise and those invited to be witnesses at weddings or other major celebrations and occasions. During the war, the soldiers — all able men between 18 and 22, who had been drafted — usually had female pen-friends who were called "war godmothers", the term arising perhaps because the war was such an important occasion: indeed, a baptism by fire. Young women, all nice daughters of good Catholic families, were almost all war-godmothers who corresponded with the soldiers so as to send them news from home and keep them company from afar. The correspondence was a way the government at the time found to mitigate the soldiers' loneliness and despair. This war correspondence was priority mail that required no postage. It was the email of the day. Sometimes, loving relationships evolved, and thus the exchange of letters between the soldiers and their lady pen-friends — their war godmothers — became something more: "flirts."

on account of the times and baptism godchildren by circumstance. For, in my orphanhood of children of my own, I had taken countless children to the baptismal font of the village church. Sons and daughters of the workers of Nothing and of the people of Ladeirinhas, many of those children were now young soldiers dragged to either the vast Angolan jungles, where UPA[43] guerrillas were butchering without rhyme or reason, or to our other overseas provinces.

During our afternoon teas Mother and I sometimes talked about the war, and I saw how weary she was of useless conflicts. With age, past memories were refreshed, and I surmised how vivid in her mind would be the long-ago farewell to Romano and the scarcity of the Second World War.

"What is this, my Daughter, other than vain glory?" she would say, her eyes focused pensively on the vague horizon and showing the fatigue of the abundance of wars her life contained. I kept silent in my complete agreement.

If ever there was a time when I felt happy for not having children, it was then. I thought about my son António, who, had he been alive, would be in his thirties and, if worse had turned to worst, might have been called to serve the nation in this, its hour of maximum greed. What things would I not have done to spare him such ultimate sacrifice, I thought. What mountains would I not have moved.

I lived the Colonial War from a distance. It was not my children dying or risking their lives in a war I knew beforehand to be lost. It was not to my house the military would be coming to get a man in the prime of life. The mother crying for a dead soldier was not I. I had already cried over my children. I had already buried them. All there was left for me now was to imagine, sympathetically, the calamity of losing a child now knocking at other doors. Naturally, I felt no relief in these thoughts, but it is always one thing to feel first-hand and

---

43. UPA. Union of the Populations of Angola, was a political anti-colonial movement founded in 1954. In 1961 it joined another anti-colonialist group to form the FNLA, National Front for the Liberation of Angola, which was one of the Angolan nationalist movements fighting in the Colonial War from 1961 to 1974.

another, totally different, to feel in the third person. I was just, and merely by a whim of fate, a third person. I was neither glad I had no children to go to war nor happy it was the children of other mothers going to war. It was all one huge waste, possible only by the insanity of those who govern.

Antero had meanwhile grown well-accustomed to Nothing. He had given up his legal practice and sold his office in Lisbon. He kept his house in Campolide, a posh neighbourhood in Lisbon, but never went there and neither did I. I did not want to intrude on the space that had once belonged to another woman. It was none of my business, and no tiniest curiosity moved me. How could I be confronted with the tastes of another woman in her own house, a house that became part of my life because I had married her widower? The mere thought of going there was morbid.

At six o'clock on an afternoon in September 1963 I heard a knocking at the door of my pantry-office. I begged come in, for I thought it to be Antero returning from the vineyards that were being harvested in yet another vintage.

My husband was a precious aide when it came to the never-ending labours of Nothing and, so like Father and Grandfather before him, he enjoyed vintage, which only made me love him more. With his help in the fields, I could have more time to concentrate on the account books and all the paperwork of Nothing.

Nobody came in.

I went to the door to see who had knocked and not ventured in. There was no one there.

Thinking I had misheard, I was resuming my seat at the desk when a faint sound of air pronouncing "Matilde" in the distance seemed to fill the room. Despite feeling an eerie chill down my spine, I made nothing of it. I had just had tea with Mother as usual and had come down to finish some paperwork before Antero came home for supper. Busy as I was, I finished what I was doing.

In the meantime, Antero got home and went upstairs to change clothes and refresh himself before we went to the dining room.

It had become our habit that when he went to our bedroom to

change I would go to the kitchen to fetch the tray with Mother's dinner. After Father and Engrácia died, I was the one who took Mother's food to her room. I refrained only from taking her breakfast, as I did not want to invade either her morning intimacies or her wanting to wake up at different hours.

Mother was lying on the bed when I entered, and the room was immersed in the half-light of falling evening.

"Here's your supper, Mother. Júlia made golden cod[44] and squash soup," I said in the banality of routine. Mother, however, made no movement. She had fallen asleep in a late nap and could not hear me.

"Mother, wake up. Supper's here," I insisted.
Seeing that Mother was still motionless, I set the tray on a low table at the bottom of the bed.

"Mother?" I called gently.

And at that precise moment I realised it.

I did not find it strange. Not in the least.

I stood there, quiet and alone. I needed a few moments before going to break the news to Antero and the rest of Nothing.

No, it was not at all strange. It was precisely twenty years to the day when Father had left us.

In her hands, resting on her lap, Mother held a picture of Father as a young man. A portrait of him by the wall of a house I did not recognise. Just as she had been his last thought in life, so too she said goodbye to this life with him on her mind. Seeing that, I realised how deep was their mutual love for each other.

Putting my hands to my mouth to muffle the sound, I wept. Regret gripped my heart for all the times I had told her she had not loved Father. Stupid. Stupid of me, who knew nothing. Stupid for only and always having thought about my own pains, while forgetting she had hers, too. In her absence from us, I was oblivious to the fact that she was no stranger to pain.

What had she felt when they told her about the young suitor who threw himself into the well because she had rejected his overtures?

---

44. Traditional fried cod recipe.

And had her mother-womb ached for the death of my children? How had my pains and losing Father hurt her?

And what had made her happy? Inasmuch as it had been so difficult to guess the feelings and sensations going through her heart, I had also never given much thought to what would have made my Mother happy. Honestly, it seemed more obvious to think about the sufferings of her life than about any joyous moments she might have experienced. Was she pleased for knowing herself to be beautiful and, when young, the object of passionate desires? Had my birth brought her any kind of bliss? What had fulfilled her?

My Mother died the same stranger she had always been to me.

In a whisper my mind triggered, I asked her softly,

"Were you proud of me, Mother?"

In my weeping, muffled by my curled palm, I let out all the sorrow I felt for not having ever known whether I had given my Mother any glimpse of happiness. Surely I had been the cause for much misery. But happiness? Had I given her some?

Pulling myself from my grief-filled thoughts, I saw her lying there, clad in a water-green crêpe Georgette dress of those she liked to wear in the 1920s, at the prime of her life, and wearing beige, spool-heeled shoes. Around her neck was her double-strand, pearl necklace and, as always, she was wearing her wedding ring and her white-gold diamond and pearl solitaire with its pavé-set, white sapphires. Her cheeks had a light kiss of rouge and her straw-blonde hair, which had never turned grey, was done in a bun tightened to her nape with a very fine, virtually invisible net, also in blonde. She smelled of *Vol de Nuit* by Guérlain, the perfume to which she had been devotedly faithful since its launch in 1933. The smell of my Mother.

On the bedside table, the hands of the clock were stopped at six.

It had all been as she wanted. There was no point in looking for suicide marks, for it was clear that if she had decided she would die that day at that hour, her will sufficed to make it so.

She eluded you.

Nor did she need me to mediate whatever mediation there might be. I was only destined to be a mere aide in the grand spectacle of her funeral, the epilogue chapter of her passing through this life, of her having lived here in this dimension.

On the walnut commode, a note, folded in two and partially open.

"To my Daughter, Luísa, everything.

Máxima"

In the expression of her last wishes, she called me, "Luísa."
Luísa.

Mother, who had baptised me Matilde, upon her dying, was calling me Luísa, thus acknowledging my personality and respecting the name Father had given me and through which I had become I.
In that note I also realised how much she loved me.
The last great and legitimate heir of Nothing was passing on to me the whole of Nothing. The last heir to have given an heir to Nothing was perpetuating it by offering me the word "everything" in testament.
The everything, I understood, was a material and emotional inheritance.
It had always been through the written word she had told me of her intense affection for me. It had been so in the letter she had sent to me in Ericeira, decades before. It was so in the note she had handwritten in the moment she prepared to voluntarily give up this life. In her strangeness, she had been a woman of profound loving, perhaps one so immensely overwhelming she could not put it into words. She just had no words to express love. Her love. She could not show that love, say the words to those she loved, for simply not knowing how.
Mother had died and, with her, we, the lineage of the blood of Nothing, were also dying. From her distanced seclusion, she was the last one to give something to Nothing.
My legacy, on the contrary, was a legacy of nothing. Nothing

would be left of me, and consequently, I could not die for Nothing to live on.

By her side, at her deathbed, I decided not to die. It was not a difficult decision to make because I had died years ago. It was simply the conscious verbalisation of the decision.

I left the room to carry the news to Antero and ask for the bells to toll.

Ever since António, the father of my son António, I had grown accustomed to giving the order for the bells to toll in the chapel of Nothing. At that hour, on that day, I was asking for the bells to toll for the last blood of Nothing, the last dead of Nothing for whom I would ever have to ask for the bells to toll.

XXVI

I buried her with all consideration and care. I did not allow an autopsy in some cold, impersonal morgue. That would desecrate her. Whole she was, whole she would forever be.

When the coffin arrived, I made sure she was placed there in the same dignified manner I had found her on the bed. I perfumed her once more with *Vol de Nuit*, straightened her clothes, and arranged her impeccable hair one last time. Then I closed the casket. Because she had seldom allowed herself to be seen in public, I would not let anyone see her in death. I was not going to have her endure that discomfort and that outrage. No one was going to remember my Mother in death because there would be no memory of that. For me, her death was peaceful.

On opening the door of the vault, I handed her over to her dearly beloved who were waiting for her. I had her placed facing the entrance, her coffin a sort of altar, so it can be her presence welcoming us when we enter, and her resting place, the first thing our eyes would see: Máxima from Nothing.

Vintage carried on as though no mourning had struck Nothing again.

I was not the recipient of anyone's sorrowful pity. There was no need for Antero to comfort me, because I was not crying. Neither was I missing Mother. Her life and her death seemed to me the most natural and sensible of things to have ever happened in Nothing. Everything regarding her had taken a perfect course and, therefore, my heart was not gloomy. And most remarkably, it was not bleeding. Over the last years, I had found peace in my relationship with her, had known her a little better in the enormity that was impossible to grasp about someone as unique as she. Our afternoon teas of few words and many silences had been worthy of a lifetime. I had regrets over nothing. Mother was a happily ended chapter in the book of my life in Nothing.

Soon after the funeral, I took up lodging in her study. I wanted to accept her gift while she might still be around, close to this dimension, before leaving for good. I wanted her to see I was entering that space to honour it.

I opened the bookcase so as to know more about her. And never, ever, have I rearranged the way she had it. The only thing that has changed is the size of the pile of my diaries, to which I kept adding, beginning with the one she as a guardian had kept for me. Not desecrating the bookcase preserved a bond of proximity with her gestures, her presence in this house. An almost imperceptible presence, and yet so overwhelming and omnipresent.

I had a desk and a chair brought in so I could work in the study. And I had a wood bookcase with diamond-shaped panes made and placed behind the desk. Whenever I sit here, I face the wall with her sacred bookcase and the faience swallows: Her, in the end.

A few months after her death, sitting here at the desk, already used to spending my afternoons in this space, I heard the seamstress there, in the corner. Distinctly. I heard the stitches, a thread being cut, the pedalling of the machine for another row of stitches.

Unafraid, I got up and neared the place where the sound was coming from. I kneeled to listen more closely. The sewing was still audible, did not stop when I stood up. Neither I nor the seamstress had frightened one another. Raising my hand gently, I stroked the air where the sound was being emitted. I wanted to touch whatever was producing it, touch a something or a someone in the unknown beyond which I was staring. A few instants later, the sound disappeared, as mysteriously as it had appeared.

Listening to the seamstress, I realised Mother was talking to me. Once, I had asked her what the sound was like, and now she had come to explain it to me. Simultaneously, I also realised that, just as I had not joined her in life because we had hardly shared a life, so too I was not to join her in death. Forever would we remain in parallel spaces that do not meet. She had been the carrier which had brought me to Nothing and to this existence, whereas I was charged with the perpetuation of here. I heard the seamstress and believed in everything.

My life went on. Never again did I hear the faint, distinct sound of a sewing machine at the corner of my study. That world, located at the interstice between here and there, was out of my reach. My rational self wanted the earth, the here and the now. And, unlike Mother, I did not possess a particular sensitivity to other worlds. It was not disbelief because, in my lack of God, and because of what I had seen of Mother's life, I believe in hereafters and other existences. It was simply a lack of dedication and little interest in opening my mind to the beyond. I knew Mother had given me a message, and my understanding of it rendered its repetition unnecessary.

As always, I focused on the Nothing inhabiting my life, which I had decided to keep and own forever. With Antero we modernised the farm.

This modernisation meant machinery: tractors, atomizers, threshers. Eventually, farm workers became scarcer and scarcer. Many young men went overseas to the colonies; others found work in the factories in Alhandra and along the railway line which headed to Lisbon. The fields were increasingly a place where nobody wanted to work. Even our beasts of burden became idle as we replaced them with machinery. Yokes of oxen and mules were put aside and kept as some sort of giant pets. Some were sold to people who still scraped a living by farming in the ancient ways. The others died of old age. All this development meant that we now administered Nothing by relying on fewer people. Paradoxically, more things got done in less time which allowed us enough freedom to spend more time sojourning in Ericeira or daring a more distant trip.

Occasionally, we would hit the road early in the morning, cross the plains of the Alentejo, and by dusk we would get to the Algarve, which by then seemed as remote as any country outside our own. As soon as my eyes spotted the iron-red soil, so unlike the grey earth of Nothing, I knew we were arriving and would look at Antero and smile in the anticipation of the good days ahead.

By then, Vale de Lobo was a salt marsh flooded by the tides, a strip of pristine nature we could cross, stepping across on the myriad pontoons and paths made with wood planks turned dark by the salty breezes and elements. Watching the crabs and the frogs in that wild environment and then arriving at the sandy beach of high dunes and foamy waves beaten by the unchained winds of the mighty Atlantic gave me immense pleasure and relaxation. For me, the Algarve was an untamed land of devil's trumpets and my bare feet on the sand.

It was around that time that I took to wearing trousers, seduced by the liberty of movement they afforded. I greatly enjoyed the clothing of that decade, just as I appreciated the air of freedom that was blowing in from everywhere. It often reminded me of Mother saying, regarding Uncle Romano, that war is a price to pay for freedom, and the more we want the latter, the greater is the cost of the war. I hoped that after all that horror, the dictatorship and the slaughtering in the colonies, a new era would dawn and with it freedom would emerge with all its debts paid. Until that day arrived, we waited and endured whatever there was to endure.

XXVII

Winter had arrived early. It had come heavy with rains, and the extensive plains leading from the southern banks of the mighty Tagus River were already flooded by the swelling Tagus waters. Nothing unusual for a place used to an abundance of water and open country that let it flow freely all around. In early autumn, the streams of Nothing had been cleared of thickets, and ditches had been opened to drain the rain. We were ready for winter and not particularly worried about the downpour, although we thought it was raining a bit more than "buckets".

"It may die down later on in the evening," I said, as I stood at the kitchen's front door, staring at the weather and the fat drops falling like a torrent from the roof, splashing loud and heavy on the paving stones in front of the porch.

"I don't know," Antero replied. "It's pouring, and I don't think it's going to stop anytime soon."

"Come on in. Get off the porch and come inside. I'm making coffee and toast," I urged, longing, as always, for his company and wanting to occupy myself with anything that would make this rainy, ugly day pass all the sooner. I wished it were time to turn in so the night could end the sadness of the day, and allow us to anticipate the possibility of waking to a sun shining brightly in the clean, clear skies that follow rains.

"I don't have a good feeling about this," said Antero as he turned to come inside. "The soils are drenched and can't absorb any more water. The springs will start bursting any second now."

"Don't fret about it. It's normal. We never get flooded here, not even if the Rio Grande and the stream overflow at the same time. Relax."

All that rain was not enough to disturb my mind. I was seasoned by the many storms that had hit Nothing throughout the years. My entire life I had faced the whims of the weather which could make or break our crops and against which there was little or nothing we could do. Once in a while there would come a year when rain was more intense, so the rivers unexpectedly overflowed their beds, but this seemed nothing so unusual as to worry us.

My soul was uplifted, though, on seeing Antero, a career and a city man, having become accustomed — I should say attached — to the rurality of my corner of the world. He had left everything for me, had come and given himself voluntarily, adapted to the country where he now lived, without regrets. Every single day I found myself fondly realising how surprised I still was at watching him, through the dispassionate eyes of the third person, being busy with the small details and the big worries of farm life. I loved him, because he loved Nothing.

We went to bed under the hammering of the downpour on the roof and the sound of water running swiftly in the gutters. That sound had always acted as a balm for my sleep in the protection and comfort that came with being the daughter of Nothing. I could rest in peace while the skies fell down, for it was a soothing, familiar feeling. I snugged against his warm body and fell asleep to the sweet sound of rain.

I wakened when I felt him sit up on the bed. I had no idea what time it was or how long had I been asleep. Half-asleep, I asked, "Are you going somewhere?"

"Go back to sleep, dear. I'm just going to check things out. I can't fall asleep with this storm."

"But are you going out in this weather? Come and lie down."

Antero had his mind set. He was like a restless dog, and I knew that against restlessness there was nothing but to act.

Unwillingly, I said goodbye to sleep.

"I'm coming with you."

I was not much in the mood for accompanying Antero into that dreadful night of water but, out of sympathy, I determined to join him, to go with him where his mind urged him to go. Nevertheless, I thought the whole thing was a complete waste of time. Totally unnecessary.

Still warmed from bed, we put on our dark-green macks and wellies, grabbed a couple of battery-operated lanterns — another sign of the modern times — and went out into the pitch-dark night. Although these were modern times, I had never got used to a mackintosh being made of plastic canvas: cold to the touch and uncomfortable. I missed the reliable oilskin of days past. Shivering with cold, we set foot off the kitchen porch and our faces were immediately washed by the pouring rain.

Antero headed to the stables that sheltered the horses and animals we had put into early retirement after the modernizing that had taken over the farm. They were dry.

Then he checked on the cellar. Dry also.

"Come, let's go back to the house. You've seen everything's alright." Frankly, I was already weary of standing out in the rain, remembering how warm and cozy were the house and our bed.

We went in, dripping and sloshing the kitchen's floor with our wet macks and muddy wellies.

We were climbing the stairs to the bedroom when we heard screams and desperate pounding at the door we had just closed.

"Help, M'am, help! The people are going to die."

Dona Eugénia, the wife of our manager, was at the door, panic written all over her fear-filled eyes.

"Help, M'am, my Joaquim and the boy have already rushed . . ." She spoke through words broken by her gasping for air.

Antero was already pulling his wellies back on. As he prepared to go back out into the rain, I listened to *Dona* Eugénia and tried to understand what was going on, knowing from her words that somewhere there were problems with furious, untamed waters.

Her husband, Senhor[45] Joaquim, *Dona* Eugénia said, and their son, who had come back from the war and had neither yet left Nothing nor given any signs of wanting to leave, had been in the tavern in Ladeirinhas. Returning home on their moped, they had seen the bridge at Amieiros, a hamlet midway between Ladeirinhas and

---

45. *Senhor*, the equivalent for Mr.

Nothing, vanish before their very eyes.

We were now isolated from the other side. She said both father and son had arrived home, warned *Dona* Eugénia, and immediately rushed on to Camargueira, a small village not far from where the Rio Grande and the Tagus met at the lake of ill omens I had imprisoned behind fences so many years before.

Antero heard "Camargueira", and, through the corner of my eye, while I finished listening to the manager's wife, I saw him go to the garage to get the jeep.

Grabbing my mack, I ran after him. It was almost midnight.

The noise was deafening. The sight, Dantean. Dark, angry water rushed by, heavy with mud and all kinds of debris, out of the banks that normally contained the Rio Grande in its course.

My husband focused on the drenched, pothole-filled macadam road, the muddy water squishing from under the weight of the tyres. Terrified, I gazed at the liquid, menacing body of water running a few steps away on our left. It looked like the lustrous, humped back of a chimeric dragon. I wanted to tell Antero to pay attention: That the river would soon get to us. As though it were possible to ask him to pay any more attention than what he was already devoting to driving in those dangerous circumstances. Not far ahead we could discern myriad lanterns whose straight, yellow beams of light were soon lost in the dark of the surrounding night. The whole village had come out into the storm.

Halting the car, we got out.

Two houses had already been carried away by the torrent. Hysterical cries of fear and panic could be heard everywhere. I had no idea whether the screams were those of people being carried away by the brutality of the water, of families trapped inside houses surrounded by the rushing streams, or of the frightened people in the street.

"Get away from here, *Dona* Luísa," yelled somebody I did not recognise, as I tried to see where Antero was going. My heart beat uncontrollably from all the horror. I saw the manager and his son, and I saw Antero join them with the quick pace of determination.

It was clear they were headed to try to save someone. I saw a man passing by, ropes in his hands, and others, running. I saw women paralysed with fear, their faces white and their eyes void of expression but for the all-encompassing terror. Children were crying with despair. I gathered into my arms one who stood, petrified, in the midst of the adults rushing by, not seeing her need. Shock had rendered her body so tense I thought I was holding a log, not a child. I left the little girl at the side of a woman who was murmuring what sounded like inarticulate prayers and headed toward the darkness where I had seen Antero vanish.

"Antero! Antero!" I called, my voice competing with the roar of the raging waters. Rain was still pouring, and the water was rising with every passing minute. For a swift instant I thought the road on which we had driven a few minutes before had already been swallowed and we were stranded.

There was a boy and a woman, maybe his mother, clinging to a half-submerged tree, its crown still above the swift current. The boy tried to seize the rope that was being thrown to them, but missed. Suddenly, the ground at the bank gave way.

I cried out.

One of the men throwing the rope to the boy was washed away. The water devoured the soil and took him in the split of a second, so sudden we barely realised what had just happened.

The distance between the land that was still safe from the deluge and the semi-submerged tree grew bigger.

Antero tried his luck at throwing the rope. There was not an instant to waste. A man had been swallowed without any hope of salvation. Two people were stuck in a tree and still alive. The attempt to rescue them could not linger in grieving for the lost rescuer.

This time the boy managed to seize the rope. He tied it around the woman's waist and pushed her into that deadly water. Immediately she was dragged away, while at the shore, a line of men headed by Antero struggled to pull her out.

I joined in the effort and realised how, because of the brute force of the water, the woman seemed to weigh tons. We pulled her out of the water, and as soon as she got to the bank, I ran to help her, while

Antero loosened the rope to throw back to the boy.

The woman was battered. Rocks and twigs and logs had ripped her clothes and bruised her body and her face. In shock, she started to throw up, and I held her head so she would not suffocate.

A cow passed by in the torrent, and I imagined flooded stables and animals in pain, drowning and dying, crushed by wrecking barns and other debris.

Behind us a collective yell announced another house had just vanished into the water. I looked at Antero, who was still throwing the rope at the boy. The sight of him calmed me. I bent down, refocusing on helping the woman.

Finally, it was the boy's turn to be in the water of that Styx. The men pulled him out with all the strength they had. He was rescued. In those brief moments, two lives saved and one lost.

I stood up to meet Antero, who was untying the rope from the boy's waist. Suddenly a something or a someone super-human pushed me by my shoulders, with such force I fell to my knees.

The ground where Antero was working had caved in. The boy, still tied to the rope, escaped.

Antero was taken away.

"Antero!" I cried.

Covered in mud and kneeling on the ground, my hands reached out for the man the water was stealing from me.

"Antero!"

XXVIII

The flood that came in the fatal night that dawned on November 26, 1967, was your swan song. Your strength, exhausted by one last scene of destructive magnificence, started to wear down from that moment on. And my life since then has been what it still is: this continuum of endless time because time is all I have and all I got from you after I had given you everything.

For some cosmic coincidence, you took hold of the downpour and the high tide to push the Tagus, already swollen by an excess of water, farther inland. In the Greater Lisbon area, the consequences were beyond devastating. People drowned while asleep at home. People were carried away by the flood when they realised what was happening and tried to get away. People died rescuing people. Cattle were lost. Houses swallowed. Crops destroyed.

For days on end I scoured the quagmires of thick, greasy silt of fertile land in search of Antero. I found dead turkeys and dogs, cows and donkeys, death-swollen like fun-fair balloons about to burst. Amidst the mud-choked and debris-filled reed beds I searched and searched. For more days than I can recall, I was all mud and desperate anxiety to find the body that made me a widow, the body I had once promised to bury as a Boshoff.

If Mother had still been here, she surely would have collected all the paper clippings that hid the true dimensions of the tragedy under the blue pen of censorship. Once the four hundred mark was reached, the government forbade further news giving the death toll. Only much later, when we were living in another era that allowed us to speak freely, did we find out the real numbers. More than seven hundred dead.

Antero was one of them.

There was, however, much jubilation in the media for the glorious solidarity that had arisen on behalf of the victims. In the news that Mother did not collect for future memory, one could read about the selfless help of the Ladies of the Feminine National Movement.

There they came, cosmopolitan in their clothes and feelings, to distribute canned sardines to those who had lost everything. In front of television cameras and photographed by journalists, they behaved to the very best of their compassionate, yet useless and vain, charity. Their benevolent gestures were celebrated and so much more important than the suffering of the tragedy-stricken and desolate populations.

The horror which had hit the plains south of the Tagus and the fields on its northern shores was rendered invisible by news saying that the deluge had its most devastating effects in Estoril, that posh village where toppled monarchs found a golden exile in their waterfront villas. Estoril had been surprised by the downpour; we were ravaged by the flood. And we, the tragedy-battered, also knew about the heartless landlords who came with police escort to collect the rents for houses which had been carried away by the raging waters. They wanted the rent of houses that were no longer there, as if the tenants were to blame for that loss of property. We knew about the corpses showing up in the ditches and canals of the Tagus, entangled in the reeds and brambles which had been left muddy and full of debris when the waters receded. We knew of the hundreds of displaced and homeless people and the famine hovering over all.

Faced with that disgraceful conduct, I felt political awareness for the first time and, just as I did, many other people must have felt it too. Maybe there is truth in the evil that comes for a greater good. The foundations of the government started to crumble in the wake of the fury of the storm that had destroyed everything. Censorship and the neglect to which the populations were subjected by all the efforts the government made to hide the people's misery became increasingly evident and far too obvious to be ignored.

In Nothing, I gave shelter to many students who came to help when everyone else had deserted us. It is perhaps our collective destiny that it took those devastating floods in all their horror to create the combination of political circumstances that led to the downfall of the dictatorship less than a decade later. If that was what it took, then Antero's death was not in vain and, again, and after Uncle Romano, my family will have given more heroes for the nation. It may be none of that, but I needed to find reasons to explain that sudden loss. Indeed, as a country looking for freedom against oppression, we owe a lot to the university students' unions, such as the University Catholic Youth, who came to our aid. Side by side with us in the quagmires, they helped us not only to dig out corpses and recover houses but also enlightened us about the paths the country should take to get out of the dictatorship. And the way was slowly being opened in the mud left by the flood and in the swamps of the government, a way towards something that was already appearing on the horizon. Yes, the students helped us and, when they left, they took with them the memory of the horror and used it to publicly denounce the offenses perpetrated by the *Estado Novo*[46] over the rural populations.

We never found Antero. For a long time afterwards I was plagued by nightmares in which I saw him drowning in the murky, foaming and furious water. I saw him struggle against the torrent, all the while swallowing the gushing water that would kill him. Frightened and soaked with perspiration, I would wake up, incapable of sleeping again, for the nightmare of loss was real.

In the many ironies of my life, António had died because of the excessive calmness of a false water, and Antero had widowed me in the wildness of water untamed. I never buried Antero. My one and only husband rests somewhere far from my life, and he may well be in a distant place, or near Nothing. He may have been taken away by the currents into the deep Atlantic, just as he may lie buried at the bottom of the Tagus. I know not. All I know is that the vault of the Boshoff, in front of which I pledged to marry him, the vault into which I invited him, will never ever receive him. In my fate as daughter of Nothing, I was first a single widow and now a widow without a husband.

After I was left without Antero, I realised I was, for the very first time, alone in the present. It was as if an amniotic sac had

---

46. *Estado Novo*, literally New State, was the name the dictatorship gave to its own rule of Portugal between 1933 and 1974.

broken, and I was being born alone. No one else connected me to the past: neither Grandfather, nor Father, nor Mother; Engrácia, nor my children. And now not even Antero. Without anyone, I was a somebody absolutely new to this life. In that so difficult labour, I was born.

And I was born, because on that night you died from me: I, from Nothing.

Epilogue

Enter carnations of a Revolution. Enter the wise and the journalists. Enter Europe[47] furnished of artificiality. The ivy covered these walls, and the palm trees started to die.[48] I survived it all. I am Máxima, the Mistress living amid the study and the bedroom in the upstairs floor of the house of Nothing. They do not disturb me. I have no idea if it is out of fear for this long thing I drag with me and which is called life or whether it is out of respect for what I am to Nothing or if it is because of my proximity to you and, as we know so well, finiteness is a human fear.

Luísa turned Mistress. Never had I thought it, never did I want it. It happened. Matilde will die out in papers and documents without anyone ever knowing who she was. She will live forever, for as long as forever has the official formality of a paper and for as long as the paper is not reduced to dust by moths and time. They no longer call me Luísa, let alone Luísa from Nothing. I hear them talking about "the Mistress" and, as so often in me, for being Matilde and Luísa, I hear of me in the third person and think of me from the outside. Who is that? Who was or am I? What will the people say about the Mistress? The people, who no longer have the memory to know of my children or my tragedies, because they were not there when all those moments were lived. The people who have never met Father nor looked in Mother's blue eyes — the eyes of Nothing. These people, unafraid of werewolves and without war for a past.

The Mistress ... She is I in this now. As I was Luísa and Lizzie and My Child and even Matilde in other nows. I fulfilled myself for what I came here to be and to do. I accepted. I mediated you. I died and I live and I live because I am going to die. I linger. I am not taking Nothing because I am nothing. Nothing remains because it is everything.

---

47. Portugal joined the European Union in 1986.

48. The bug attacking palm trees, *Rhynchophorus ferrugineus*, is a plague introduced in Portugal in 2007 and responsible for the death of thousands of palm trees in the Mediterranean region.

A Chronology of Portuguese History Intersecting with the Story of Nothing

1807–1810 – French Invasions. In 1807, a French army commanded by General Jean-Andoche Junot, under the orders of Napoleon, marches through Portugal and reaches the capital, Lisbon, on November 30. The Portuguese King, João VI, and the entire Court had meantime fled to Brazil, then a Portuguese colony, to avoid surrendering to the invaders. Two other invasions followed, in 1808 and 1810. Around Lisbon, a line of forts, called *Linhas de Torres*, were built to protect the general population and to thwart the advances of the French armies. While the Court was in Brazil, Portugal was administered by a Council headed by British Marshal William Carr Beresford.

1908 – Portuguese King Carlos I and Crown Prince Afonso are killed by Republican sympathisers, and the King's younger son is proclaimed King Manuel II.

1910 – A Republican coup topples the Monarchy and King Manuel II is forced into exile with the Royal Family. He would die in London in 1932.

April 9, 1918 – Battle of Lys, known in Portugal as Battle of La Lys, was the heaviest military defeat by Portuguese forces since the Battle of Ksar El-Qibir in Morocco in 1578 and a decisive Portuguese intervention in World War I. The Second Division of the Portuguese Expeditionary Corps, commanded by General Gomes da Costa, faced the offensive commanded by German General Ferdinand von Quast. Hundreds of Portuguese soldiers were lost in action or taken prisoners. Many of the soldiers came from the areas around Lisbon.

1933–1974 – A Fascist regime, under the leadership of António de Salazar, seizes power, beginning the era also known as the Second Republic or Estado Novo (New State). Civil rights, such as free speech, freedom of assembly and elections, were abolished. A police state, PIDE, the *Polícia de Intervenção e Defesa do Estado* (State Intervention and Defense Police) was created to control any attempts at insurrection. Thousands of political prisoners were sent to jail, either in Portugal or exiled and held in inhumane prison facilities in the African colonies.

1936–1939 – Spanish Civil War. Despite an agreement for non-direct intervention, the Portuguese regime was supportive of the Francoist dictatorship. In 1936, Spanish Republican refugees crossed the border into Portugal near the village of Barrancos in the south of Portugal, thus creating a diplomatic incident by which Portuguese authorities, sympathising with the Spanish regime, were asked to return the refugees to Spain, where they were to be tried and sentenced. The incident sullied Portugal in the eyes of the foreign press and international community which accused the country of collaborating with an authoritative regime.

1939–1945 – Second World War. In 1939, Salazar's government declared the country's neutrality in the conflict, a position it maintained until the end of the war, despite accepting many Jew refugees. In fact, the official policy was that Jews could enter the country to avoid persecution, but they could not stay indefinitely so as not to jeopardise the country's pact of non-belligerence. In Portugal, the consequences of the war were mostly felt in the rationings imposed on the population.

February 15, 1941 – A rare hurricane hits Portugal, leaving a trail of devastation in its wake. It was felt most heavily around midday in the Lisbon area.

1961–1974 – Portuguese Colonial War, or *Guerra do Ultramar*. In the wake of independence movements throughout Africa in the 1950s and 1960s, Portuguese African colonies, namely Angola, Mozambique and Guinea-Bissau, engaged in a war for self-determination against the metropolis, that is, in empire and imperialism studies terms, Portugal, as the power that held these overseas colonies. After a series of incidents involving the taking of the prison in Luanda, Angola, and a tribal uprising in which white settlers in the hinterland of Angola were killed, the Portuguese government deployed military contingents to the colonies in an effort to preserve the overseas territories within the sphere of the Portuguese empire. The war ended in 1974, as a consequence of the April Revolution, and the colonies were granted independence soon after.

November 25, 1967 – Heavy rainfall causes some of the worst floods in history to have affected the Greater Lisbon area. Many lives were lost and the tragedy highlighted the miserable living conditions of people in the lower socioeconomic population. Censorship forbade the press from covering the true damage the floods had caused. The actual number of victims was known only after the Revolution of 1974.

April 25, 1974 – The Movement of Armed Forces, led mostly by army Captains who had served in the Colonial War, marched into Lisbon to overthrow the Fascist regime. The rebellious army battalions were welcomed by Lisboans who gathered in the streets of the capital and gave the soldiers carnations. The flowers later became the symbol of a revolution with no loss of life. The government toppled, its leaders were sent to exile in Brazil, and the prisons were opened to free the thousands of political opponents who had been incarcerated and tortured by PIDE.

1986 – Portugal joins the European Union as a free democratic country.